Billie Standish was HERE

Billie Standish was HERE

NANCY CROCKER

Simon & Schuster Books for Young Readers

New York · London · Toronto · Sydney

SIMON & SCHUSTER BOOKS FOR YOUNG READERS · An imprint of Simon & Schuster Children's Publishing Division · 1230 Avenue of the Americas, New York, New York 10020 · This book is a work of fiction. Any references to historical events, real people, or real locales are used fictitiously. Other names, characters, places, and incidents are products of the author's imagination, and any resemblance to actual events or locales or persons, living or dead, is entirely coincidental. · Copyright © 2007 by Nancy Crocker · All rights reserved, including the right of reproduction in whole or in part in any form. · SIMON & SCHUSTER BOOKS FOR YOUNG READERS is a trademark of Simon & Schuster, Inc. · Book design by Alicia Mikles · The text for this book is set in Bembo. · Manufactured in the United States of America · 10 9 8 7 6 5 4 3 2 1 · CIP data for this book is available from the Library of Congress. · ISBN-13: 978-1-4169-2423-4 · ISBN-10: 1-4169-2423-X

FIRST
EDITION

To Dan

Chapter One

My name is Billie Standish. William Marie Standish.

It's pretty clear what my parents' expectations were.
The "Marie" was a nod to Daddy's mother because she
died two months before I was born. Otherwise, who
knows? I might have been William Edward.

My parents were told at my birth there would be no
more babies. So you might say my name was down payment for using up their one chance to have a son.

For a long time I was mostly invisible. That was okay,
though. Once you've figured out you can't do anything
right it's just good sense not to call undue notice your
way. Why step out of the shadows and get yelled at for
blocking somebody's light?

Besides, my mama's always had the kind of temper
that gets the nearest dog kicked once in a while just for
being there. Being invisible had its benefits.

My parents are farmers like most folks around Cumberland, so it wasn't hard to stay out of sight. Working to cobble together a living between what little land they owned and what they could rent didn't exactly get them home for weekends and paid vacations.

Most families either had sons or made do with fewer acres. Not ours. Mama rode a tractor as many hours as Daddy, and they worked as much ground as any two people could. It had them gone early and home late and dog tired pretty much year-round, but it also kept us living at least a little better than some. I didn't have to go home from school at lunchtime and eat potatoes or cold cereal like some kids did.

We weren't rich by anybody's yardstick. I knew better than to ask for new clothes unless my shoes were absolutely too tight or the queen of England was invited to our house for supper. But I always went back to school in the fall with new stuff. I had a few extras. I had enough.

Providing enough and having a girl instead of a boy had put a lot of calluses on Mama's hands, though, and she was willing to grant me title of ownership to every single one of them. She could work in the fields, I couldn't. Her call, but my fault. There's no figuring it out. Believe me, I've tried.

You'd think free maid service would count for something, but it never seemed to pay down my account even a little bit.

They say I stayed with my Grandma Wharton a lot when I was little, but she died when I was seven and I barely remember. I've mainly been on my own since then when Mama and Daddy are gone planting, gone cultivating, gone harvesting. Gone plowing or mending fences. Just gone.

Nothing much bigger than a silent fart can get past the neighbors in a town this size, though, so I suppose I was looked after in a way.

The summer of 1968, I was eleven years old. The last day of school was May 24 and also the fifth day in a row I walked home in a bone-soaking rain. I had to strip to the skin and hang my wet stuff on the clothesline strung across the back porch before I went on into the house. And then find something to do. Find anything to do. Fill enough hours to keep from feeling alone as a castaway washed up on a deserted island.

A week after the last day of school the house was spotless and the television was making a funny whining noise after it ran for a couple of hours. I had memorized every freckle and measured the progress of every pimple on my face. And it was still raining.

Cats and dogs. Lizards and groundhogs. A real toad-strangler. A gully-washer. I spent part of one afternoon thinking up all the stupid nicknames for rain that I could and then I dragged out the Bible and read the story of Noah all the way down to the rainbow. When I was done the clock next to my bed told me I still had three more hours to fill before time to cook supper.

Labor Day was at least a lifetime away from that first week of June.

The fourth of the month, a Tuesday, Mama shook me awake just after dawn. She said, "This goes to the back door," and handed me a key. "If you go outside today—and I *do* wish you'd at least get the mail for once—lock the house."

Mama's tongue is sharp enough to wedge criticism into any remark.

I mumbled, "Why?" Then I pulled the covers over my head and mouthed the answer along with her.

"Because I said so."

I knew that. It was the explanation for everything she told me to do. What I hadn't known was that the back door even had a lock. To my knowledge it had never been used in my lifetime.

I could see her with my eyes closed, slicing the air with her hip bones and elbows as she crossed me off the list in her head and moved on. Another chore taken care of.

I listened for both pickup doors to slam, Mama-*Daddy*, then jumped up and threw on shorts to go with the panties and T-shirt I'd slept in. I raked my hair back in front of the dresser mirror long enough to see that the zit on my right cheek was the size of Mount Olympus, same as the day before.

I had pretty much lived behind my bedroom door the past couple of weeks. It felt safer somehow than rattling around loose in the house by myself, and the big mirror across the back of my dresser was there any time I needed a reminder that I existed. Even so, when I got to the back porch and was locked in I thought I'd suffocate before I figured out the latch. There's a big difference between a cave and a cage—ask any lion at the zoo.

I hurdled the back step and ran like the house was trying to swallow me. It still wasn't easy to breathe and, while I stood in the middle of the driveway working on that, I noticed something else not right.

The snot-nosed brats weren't fighting in the yard next door, even though the sun was shining for the first time in weeks. It was pretty muddy, sure, but I'd seen that woman line 'em up and hose 'em down at the end of the day rather than keep them inside with her.

I couldn't hear any cars either, so I shut my eyes to listen. A few anemic birds were chirping, but that was it. In Cumberland, *somebody's* dog is *always* barking. But not that day.

I went to the front hedge and looked up and down

the street, and it might have been a painting. Even the trees were still, leaves too wet and heavy to move.

I'd seen *Candid Camera* on TV and it felt like I was in the middle of some practical joke. But people trying to make a living off row crops just don't waste time pulling pranks on the neighbors' kids. I knew that.

I went back and locked the door, then started walking down the middle of the street so I'd see anything that started my way. I like a scary movie now and then, but I always hate the jump-out-and-grab-somebody scenes.

I would guess most little towns in Missouri are past their heydays. In Cumberland's case, a bunch of burnt-out skeleton buildings along Main Street stand ready to testify that the town has seen better times. A handful of empty houses gone to seed, a few scattered vacant lots—they're just different parts of the same story. Cumberland isn't exactly material for picture magazines anytime, but it looked downright spooky that day.

That day *every* house I passed looked to be abandoned. Dingy little boxes, most of them needing fresh white paint ... an occasional outburst of aluminum siding in some color that would startle God. No sign of life in any window.

Most of the lots in town are fenced into little chain-link prison yards for all creatures under three feet tall. All that individual territory staked out looked really ridiculous with nobody around.

It doesn't take long to walk the town, and I did all four blocks by four blocks without sharing air with anything but birds and squirrels.

I got to the schoolhouse, then walked around to the playground and sat down in a swing where I could see the state blacktop that swipes the west edge of town. Ten minutes or so went by without one single person passing through.

The thought occurred that maybe I should be afraid, but that's not exactly something you *decide* and there just wasn't anything real to wrap fear around. It was pretty clear there was nothing around to jump out at me. This wasn't like any movie I'd ever seen.

The world had turned inside out. Overnight. Or at least during the ten days I'd spent in my cocoon. Everybody else had disappeared and left me exposed.

Sitting there in that swing, I started to feel like I might shrink as the sky grew wider and the sun stared me down. I had to get up and move before I got stuck in the moment and it went on forever. I could be a speck of dust in no time.

I started to recite as I walked past houses a second time: The Millers and the Statons and the Hises, the Athertons and the McCombses . . . I just saw Mama this morning. I just saw Mama this morning.

A shiver ran down my back.

I peeked in a couple of windows on the way home and sure enough, all the furniture was gone. The doors were locked, too, so there wasn't much to do but keep walking.

I tried to remember if I'd heard more trucks than usual driving around town, but that was like trying to recollect how many times in the last week a train had gone through and rattled the windows. It was such an ordinary sound I wouldn't notice. Mama was right—I should have at least left the house to get the mail once in a while. There sure hadn't been any announcements on the transistor radio in my room. And the girl in the mirror hadn't told me anything.

I was about to turn up our driveway when somebody yelled my name, and I must have jumped a couple of feet.

Lydia Jenkins was in the flower garden back of her house across the street. I didn't know her very well but I guess I was pretty glad to see her just the same.

She was old even then so it took her a while to get across the garden. She looked like every grandma in the world—a lumpy flowered cotton dress cinched in the middle with a belt, legs shapeless as tree trunks hobbling along over the uneven ground, using her hoe for a cane. She leaned on the fence, squinted her wrinkles at the sky and said, "Lordy, Lordy. If I was to be asked, I'd say it's about time we had some sun, wouldn't you?"

I said, "Yeah, I guess," then blurted out, "Where is everybody, Miss Lydia?"

She laughed like it was a joke. "Why . . . gone, Billie Marie." She always called me that when we spoke, even though everybody else just called me Billie. She told me, "The Millers and the Corlews were the last to go, just yesterday. Suppose it's only you folks and me 'n' Curtis now."

I didn't say anything and she appeared to search my face. "Surely you noticed? People been loadin' up and movin' out for pretty near two weeks now."

I shook my head. "Nobody told me."

She laughed again and my cheeks started burning. "Well, lands, child, nobody told you put one foot in front of the other this mornin' if you wanted to walk, either, did they?"

I was ashamed for speaking up and a little mad—two more reasons not to do it very often. "Well," I said, "am I supposed to know *why*, too?"

She looked sorry then. "No, I suppose not. I forget you're just a child, you've grown so." She moved her hoe handle so she could lean on it with both hands. "Your folks ain't said nothin' at all?"

I shook my head.

Miss Lydia took that in, then nodded. "People's afraid the levee's gonna break. Think it's gonna be '51 all over again." She wasn't looking at me anymore.

"Well, is it?" My heart started thumping. "I mean, why are we still here? Why are you?"

Miss Lydia smiled just a small smile. "You're right, somebody should've told you." She looked to the south, toward the river. "Well, your daddy 'n' me seem to have better memories than most. And we recall it took a full twenny-four hours after the levee broke in '51 for the water to get to town. That's a whole lotta time if you make every bit of it count. I reckon he figures his time right now is better spent sandbaggin' levees unless he's just *gotta* get you all out. And me, well . . ." She snorted and her face knotted up. "You know my boy Curtis is back livin' with me, don't you?"

I nodded.

"Even a man who won't take out the garbage can usually find time to be a hero," she went on. "I expect I'll have help if I need it."

I tried to sort it all out even as it was still sinking in. I had supposed Mama and Daddy were in the field every day like always, not shoring up levees against the river. I don't ask questions when they come in too tired to do much more than grunt hello at me, but the truth was I hadn't even considered what all that rain pounding the house added up to. Stupid.

I felt like I needed some little redemption in her eyes, so I said, "Hey, I'm gonna walk up and get the mail in a while. Want me to bring you yours?"

Miss Lydia gave me a good look at her false teeth then. "Why, that'd be right nice of you." I'd only gotten a couple of steps toward home when she yelled. I turned around. "Bring it by about noon and we'll have some dinner together."

I would have rather gone to church in shoes two sizes too small. I could sit on the fringe of a conversation and nod once in a while, but I didn't know how to make chitchat with anybody—and *especially* somebody who could remember when God was a boy. "Oh no, Miss Lydia, you don't need to—"

"Don't need to. Want to." She looked up and down the street. "Just you 'n' me, you know. Curtis is in the city most of the time, even now that he's back. May as well keep a little company."

I nodded, then ran home—gravel, bare feet, and all. I shut the door to my room and sat on the bed to think. There had been a note from Daddy on the kitchen table a few mornings that summer, telling me the Corps of Engineers would be calling later and to write down a message when they did. But he hadn't volunteered what the numbers in those messages meant, and of course I hadn't asked.

I thought about Daddy and Miss Lydia calculating how much twenty-four hours could buy and wondered when they had talked. I couldn't remember the last time Daddy had said anything directly to me. Sometimes he seemed surprised to notice me at all—like he'd forgotten again that it wasn't just him and Mama.

I lay back on the bed, adding up the inventory of everything below doorknob level in our house and picturing it all piled in the bed of a grain truck. It wouldn't take that long to load. So why was everybody else gone? They had to know something.

Unless Daddy was the only soldier in the parade marching to the right drummer. He never had trouble believing that. If all the other farmers were planting soybeans fence post to fence post, he'd decide to put in winter wheat and follow it with hay. If everybody else was rushing to get the corn in when it was still a little damp, he'd take a chance on the weather and leave it in the field till it was dry.

One time I looked up at a V of geese flying and saw one straggler off to the side, determined to go it alone even if he had to flap twice as hard. That was Daddy. Every gaggle I've seen fly over since has made me think of him.

Thing is, he's usually right. Or at least far enough into the gray area that you couldn't call him wrong. About the time he's selling that hay crop, a hailstorm comes along and wipes out everyone else's beans. He ends up getting five cents a bushel more for his corn than all those who picked theirs wet. It's hard to say how much is smart and how much is luck, but I've never known anybody to change Daddy's mind once it was made up, so there was no point thinking about it. If he had decided we'd wait out the rain, I knew we would.

Then that comment Miss Lydia had made about a man finding time to be a hero came back to me. Talking about her son Curtis. He'd for sure be the one who wouldn't take out the garbage.

When you hang around like a shadow, you know people mainly by what you overhear. That's how I knew Curtis. And what I'd heard was that Curtis couldn't find his ass with both hands. If it was on fire. And he had a map. Wink Sweeney said one time that Curtis was mainly a smart aleck, but without the smart part.

Curtis had been back since the middle of May. He was in his early forties and, if what I'd heard was true, he turned up at Miss Lydia's door every five or ten years and stayed till she put him out a few months later. Somebody said he showed up whenever he got out of jail, but that seemed doubtful. He'd have had to commit crimes on another planet for nobody in Cumberland to come forward with any particulars.

This time he had a job in Kansas City working at the Ford plant. I'd heard folks talking about it one day when

I stopped in for a Coke at the store attached to the grain elevator. The lunch counter in there served up more news and gossip than it did sandwiches.

Daddy was having coffee with the men that day and offered his opinion that Curtis wouldn't last six months at Ford.

Dolores Swank was wiping the counter with a rag and told Daddy to give Curtis a break, you couldn't expect him to be "right" after that accident killed the only girlfriend he ever had. But when Daddy shot back with the reminder that Curtis had been ass-over-teakettle drunk and driving the car when that girl got killed, nobody said another word.

I'd never devoted Lydia Jenkins a whole lot of thought before and I tried to gather together everything I knew about her. Evidently Daddy respected her enough to compare notes on the weather. That was something.

I decided she most likely hadn't been raised in Cumberland. When I thought about it, people were just a little too polite to Miss Lydia for her to be a native. They "yes, ma'ammed" and "no, ma'ammed" her, something you don't hear all the time.

But some of that could be because she was mother to Curtis too. Nobody in our neck of the woods would dare point a finger at the family tree of any bad apple—lest one of his own turn rotten somewhere down the road.

But farm folk do tend to act like bad luck might be contagious, and one way to gain a little distance is with an extra layer of sugar coating. Curtis was probably worth a whole lot of "ma'ams."

The more I thought, though, the more sure I was the Jenkinses came from elsewhere. Mama had never mentioned any of Curtis's wrongdoings growing up and that meant they hadn't gone to school together. She could recite a catalog of every misstep her schoolmates had ever made and was never shy about doing it.

I knew Miss Lydia's husband had passed sometime in the last ten years and she had a green thumb with the gladioli.

That was about it. Not more than a sketch and a guess or two. I'd just have to try and make it through lunch without doing anything too stupid.

At ten to noon I locked the house again and walked up to the little shack that had been our post office as long as I could remember. Lewis McEntire barely looked up when I started twirling the combination on our box. He just grunted when I asked for Miss Lydia's mail, and already had his nose back in somebody's new *Reader's Digest* when he slid her bundle under the grate at the window.

It was kind of like at home when I wasn't looking in the mirror. Like I wasn't really there.

Chapter Two

But I sure was accounted for at Miss Lydia's. I could hear her singing "Little Red Wing" while I wiped my feet at the back step, and when she threw open the door it was like a party started. She had fried a chicken and made potatoes with milk gravy and she pointed me toward a paring knife and a pyramid of tomatoes while she took up the food. And she kept on singing.

Then she took the platter of tomatoes from me and said it looked pretty as a picture. That started my ears to burn because I knew Mama would have complained that the slices were ragged and I didn't peel them. Funny how she could criticize me even when she wasn't there.

I couldn't remember the last time I'd sat down to a table. I ate alone in front of the TV before my folks got home at night, then went to my room after I told them hello and reheated what I'd cooked.

Miss Lydia sat across from me and, after we'd exhausted just about everything that could be said about the weather, she started telling stories about people in town. I only knew them as grown-ups, but she knew a lot of the boneheaded things they'd done when they were kids. And her stories sounded funny, not mean. She wasn't looking to cut anybody down.

She told me one she said she'd heard from my Grandma Standish—how my dad and a bunch had it up to play a prank on Mr. McCombs one Halloween, but somebody tipped the mean old so-and-so off. So when Daddy stepped foot on his front porch, the old man's voice rang out in the dark: "Okay, men, shoot to kill."

I was taking a drink when she said that Daddy nearly shit his drawers, and I laughed so hard lemonade came out my nose. But she didn't get mad. She just handed me a paper towel and laughed along with me. I wasn't used to anything like it.

I wasn't used to talking so much, either, but once my lid popped open the words just seemed to spill out. Like when Miss Lydia motioned me to dab at the corner of my mouth and I explained that was a scar and didn't wipe off. She asked how I got it and, without even thinking, I told the whole story—how we were all driving to church one Sunday when I was five and I asked when I was going to have a baby sister or brother. How Mama reached over the seat to backhand me and her ring caught, just at the corner of my mouth.

Miss Lydia looked as shocked by my question as Mama had been. But all she said was, "It cut deep enough to leave that scar?"

I told her, "Oh, no. But it got kinda infected and that made it worse."

I had said too much, judging by the way she was staring at her lap. And I wanted so bad for her to still like me. "I was just a little kid then," I told her. "I know better now than to ask grown-ups about their personal business like that."

She looked up and said, "Yes, I suspect you do." Then she asked if I had seen Ed Sullivan Sunday evening, and I was pretty sure everything was still okay between us.

While I was drying the dishes after lunch, she stopped with her hands in the soapsuds and turned to me like she'd just had a big idea. The way things turned out, I guess she had.

"How'd you like to earn a little pin money?" she asked.

I shrugged.

"Seems to me it wouldn't hurt to get the house a little bit ready, just in case the river's got different ideas than your daddy does. And I got too much junk settin' around anyway. How about helpin' me wrap up some of my knickknacks and haul 'em upstairs in boxes?"

Miss Lydia had one of the few two-story houses in town. That little fact seemed quite a bit more important now, with the river flexing its muscles six short miles away.

"Uh-huh," I said, "sounds pretty smart to me."

"No need to tell your daddy, of course," she said and she winked. "I don't suppose even with the two of us we could move the furniture . . . ."

"Couldn't Curtis do that for you?"

Miss Lydia shot me a look that would've made a big dog tuck his tail. I dropped the glass I was drying and my face went hot while I stuttered how sorry I was.

"So am I," she said. We knelt down together to pick up the big pieces, then she went for the broom and handed it to me. When she emptied the dustpan into the waste-basket, she started humming "Red Wing" again. Something had happened, but I didn't understand what.

She came back to the sink smiling at me and brushed the hair out of my eyes just like Mama used to do when I was little and cute. We didn't talk anymore until after we had finished the dishes and started wrapping and packing her stuff.

Things being pretty dusty in an old person's house, we decided we might as well wash everything before we wrapped it, so we had barely made a dent when her clock chimed seven and I said I needed to go home and start thinking about supper.

"You're a good'un," she said. But it was the second time that day she lost her smile. She got her purse and handed me two dollars.

"Oh, Miss Lydia, that's too much."

She shook her head. "'T'isn't."

"You fed me." I held one dollar out to her.

She finally smiled again. "Fair enough. How about tomorrow, then? Still plenty to do."

I said, "Sure, what time?" and she said if I'd bring her the mail at noon, we'd start right over like it was yesterday. I was almost asleep much later when I remembered I hadn't needed to look in the mirror all day.

The next morning I took my first bath in a week and washed my hair. I guess even a castaway tries to clean up when he finally sees a ship on the horizon. I'd been wearing the same shorts and shirt for nearly that long, so I stuffed them into the bathroom hamper and pulled the last fresh clothes out of my dresser. I had been saving them for some reason, and it seemed like this must be it.

With a little shine to it dry and brushed, I saw my hair almost had what you could call highlights. Huh. Usually it just looked the color of mud. Something about the light made my eyes look greener than usual, too. The Mount Olympus of zits didn't look quite as angry as the day before and hadn't invited any friends to join it. I dabbed on a little concealer and managed a smile for the mirror. I didn't look half bad, for me.

Miss Lydia had cooked ham steaks, fried potatoes, and green beans. It all tasted better than anything I'd ever had. She even complimented me on my appearance.

I said "thank you," then said, "But I'm afraid this is about the end of the clean clothes. Mama just hasn't been home . . . ."

"Well, why can't you do it? You allergic to laundry soap?"

For some reason that struck me so funny I started giggling hard enough to pee my pants. Almost. Then Miss Lydia got tickled at *me* laughing. We were both wiping our eyes before we could quiet down.

I remember every little thing because it felt strange to be laughing so much. In my folks' house, you'd have thought laughter was an expensive commodity. Payable per use.

Finally I was able to answer. "No . . . I offered to, but Mama told me to stay away from the wringer. I don't know how to run it and she doesn't want to come home and find me tangled up in it, bleeding to death. She says that's all she needs."

Miss Lydia laid her fork down. "Well, you just march yourself over there after dinner and bring those clothes over here. I can sure as hell show you how to push the buttons on my machine."

I was flabbergasted. Not at her swearing—that didn't even register until later. I gurgled trying to get the words out. "You got an automatic?" Mama had told me we couldn't have one because Cumberland had no town water line for it to drain into.

"Yessir. Best thing I ever bought." She thought for a minute. "'Cept maybe the color TV."

I was used to feeling in the way whenever anybody could see me, but just then I felt three times the size of an elephant. "I'm here to help you, not make you do our work," I told her.

"Land' a livin', child," she laughed. "You don't put the clothes in and set there watchin' 'em go around for half an hour. I expect we can do both things. Bring your own soap, if it'll make you feel better."

I did seven loads while we worked that afternoon and Miss Lydia seemed pleased watching me fold clean clothes into boxes to carry home. When I came back for the hamper, she asked what I was cooking that night.

"Oh, salmon cakes, probably. We're pretty much down to canned and frozen stuff."

"You can fry a chicken, can't you?"

I thought so. "But I don't know how to cut one up," I told her.

Her eyes started shining. "Well, you lay one out to thaw tonight, and bring it over here when you come tomorrow at noon. Ain't had a chicken outsmart me yet."

That was the last discussion we had about me coming back. After that we just assumed I would.

Mama started to bawl me out that night for going near the wringer, but after I explained what I'd really done she didn't know what to say. All the while she put clean clothes away she kept opening her mouth and then changing her mind, like she was arguing with herself. Open, shut, open, shut. She looked like a big fish that wasn't happy but wasn't sure why.

I had hidden the frozen chicken under my bed before she got home, which felt kind of stupid even as I did it. But I'd never fried a chicken before and didn't want to be criticized in advance of trying. Mama could warn me not to make a mess, not to waste anything, not to ruin something, not to not do anything with so much authority I sometimes felt like I couldn't blink without screwing *that* up.

So she was positively wary of me the following night when she came home to fried chicken with all the fixings warm on the stove. I hadn't shown my hand before it was played—and hard as she looked around she couldn't find anything in the results to complain about.

I was starting to feel like I was there, even in my own

house. Even when my parents were around.

I was way past knocking at Miss Lydia's when the day came that I got the surprise of Curtis sitting at the kitchen table. An empty Coke and a full ashtray sat in front of him and he looked up from the newspaper through a stinky blue haze. I stood there just inside the door.

He said, "Well, hello there," and his face split into a grin. His teeth were yellow and he seemed to have more of them than most people did. The smell of smoke made my stomach churn.

I wondered where Miss Lydia was and if I should leave. About the time he said, "What's a matter? Cat got your tongue?" and started laughing at his genius originality, Miss Lydia appeared at the foot of the stairs out in the hallway.

When she saw me she hurried in as fast as she could, which meant it seemed like it only took a month. She had some papers in her hand and started swatting at the air.

"Lord, Curtis, how many times I told you I don't want you smokin' in here?" She quick-hobbled over to the window above the sink, cranked it open, and started fanning her apron like she was scooping the dirty air outside.

"Well, now, Ma, I got to stop taking orders from you

right around the time I turned free, white, and twenty-one," Curtis drawled. He winked at me while he clasped his hands and stretched his arms above his head.

Miss Lydia harrumphed at the stove, then turned and set a full plate in front of him. "Curtis appears to have the day off work and has decided to grace us with his presence," she told me, "so would you get silverware for all of us, please?" And one second after she sliced those words off the edge of a tight little smile, she threw him the hateful look I'd seen once before. The one that had made me drop a glass and break it.

Then she turned and started filling the next plate.

I swallowed the bile rising in my throat. This was worse than home with Mama in one of her moods and I didn't know if I could choke down food at a table with the two of them.

I was trying to conjure up an exit line when Miss Lydia said, "Billie Marie?" Both of them were looking at me, waiting. I got the forks and knives, dealt them out, and slid into my chair.

It was a different house. Miss Lydia was tuned up tight as a fiddle string and I was vibrating in close harmony. My knuckles went white holding my fork and I wasn't doing much with my plate but rearranging it. Miss Lydia looked to be doing the same. She kept her eyes down and never looked at Curtis again before he left.

He ate faster than any person I've ever seen, but even so, his manners were neat almost to the point of finicky. Outside of TV, I had never seen anyone raise their pinky as they lifted their glass and I never could have imagined it with a dirty fingernail. For all his hurry, I didn't see a speck of food go anywhere it shouldn't, and his napkin was a white flash between his mouth and his lap.

For some reason, I remembered the wolf in "Little Red Riding Hood," who put on clothes and talked and was a good enough imitator to pass for a human being. That had scared the bejeezus out of me as a little kid.

Nobody had said another word when Curtis laid his folded napkin beside his plate and stood up. He took one last drink of tea, pushed his chair in, cleared his throat and said, "Ladies." Without looking at either of us, he stalked out the back door as hunch-shouldered and bowlegged as any cowboy heading into the wind.

Miss Lydia closed her eyes for about five seconds, then opened them and smiled. "Clear that plate for me, would you?" She nodded toward Curtis's place. "I'd do it myself, but my food would be cold by the time I got myself up and back into my chair." We both chuckled and I jumped up and piled his place setting in the sink.

When I sat down again, it was like nobody else had been there. Miss Lydia made some comment about the weather and we fell to talking like we always did while we ate. Things were back to normal until I asked in the course of things when it was that she had moved to Cumberland.

Just like that the air was almost too thick to take in and Miss Lydia seemed frozen, staring at the spot Curtis had occupied. Her mouth moved without sound like she was trying on words. I didn't know what to do—it had seemed like such a nothing question.

Her words came slowly. "Mr. Jenkins inherited this house about the time Curtis left for college." She cleared her throat. "It seemed like a good time for a fresh start. . . ."

Curtis went to college? Maybe I wondered out loud, because she went on to say, ". . . for three months. Then he showed up here one weekend . . . there was an accident. . . ."

I tried to help her along. "The one with the girl."

She nodded and it was all there on her face.

My heart was pounding to beat the band and I knew I should change the subject, but I just had to ask. "But why . . . Miss Lydia, why do you take him in?"

She shook her head. "Guilty conscience, I suppose." She looked at me with eyes that held no life.

I started sputtering. "Oh, but Miss Lydia, no—you— I mean, it's not—"

She waved her hand halfheartedly. "No, I know I

didn't do right by him. Not ever. I'm not proud, but it's God's own truth." Her bottom lip was stretched to a thin white line.

I couldn't imagine how somebody as good as Miss Lydia could think she had done wrong by somebody as ornery as Curtis. But whatever she was remembering was about to make her cry, and I wasn't about to ask anything that might knock a hole in that dam. So I did change the subject then.

I stared at my bedroom ceiling that night thinking about how every single person on earth, no matter who they turned into later, started out as somebody's baby.

Everybody started out a blessing or a disappointment. A prayer that had been answered or nothing more than another mouth to feed. All by the time they'd drawn their first breath.

I tried to imagine Miss Lydia with a little baby and had a hard time believing she wouldn't do right by him. Didn't she rock Curtis and sing lullabies and think he might grow up to be president? Didn't she teach him nursery rhymes and ring-around-the-rosy?

I could only imagine what might have made a fresh start in Cumberland seem like a good idea to Miss Lydia. Then, within three months, Curtis had brought shame and scandal down on her house. I wondered just how much fuel was in those looks of hers that could burn down a house. What a woman like Miss Lydia felt when her baby grew up to be a . . . a Curtis. And why she would blame herself.

I didn't know then. But I did start to see better why Miss Lydia was being so nice to me. Women like her always seem to need someone to mother. And it was pretty clear her first pass at it hadn't turned out very well for anybody.

Of course there was also the fact I was about as close to a motherless child as she was going to find.

The next morning around eleven, I was home alone like usual when someone started banging on the back door. The way our house is situated, when you step out onto the back porch anybody at the door can see you at the same time you see them. That had never mattered to me until I went out and found Curtis Jenkins grinning in at me.

I jumped back and hollered through the kitchen doorway, "What do you want?"

He snorted. "Well, hello to you, too."

"Hello, Curtis. What do you want?" I said.

"Can I come in and use your phone?"

Maybe it was because I had spent so much time the night before pondering why and when he'd turned out like he had, but my ears started ringing.

"How come you want to use our phone?" I asked him. Stall. Think. Clang clang clang.

"Ours is out," he grinned. "Guess all this rain has the lines down somewhere."

I said, "Sorry. Ours is out, too," and I saw a tiny flicker of surprise in his eyes. He had been lying.

His forearm was leaned against the door facing, and now he pushed off with it and took a step back. "Well, you don't know how sorry I am to hear that," he said and turned to go, ducking his head against the rain.

Miss Lydia asked me three times that afternoon why I was so quiet, but I couldn't bring myself to tell her. It wasn't like anything had actually happened, and I figured she didn't need to feel any worse toward Curtis. I decided to forget about it in my sleep that night and wake up happy.

I could still do that then.

Chapter Three

*M*iss Lydia and I finished cleaning her knick-knacks and storing them upstairs. It could have been done in three afternoons, but it took nine because she stopped to tell me the story behind each porcelain figure and engraved souvenir. Mr. Jenkins had worked for the railroad and traveled most of the time up until he retired and Miss Lydia had traveled with him a lot back in the early days of their marriage. It seemed like a lot, anyway, to somebody who had only been to Kansas City three times.

They'd been to Denver and New York City and took a steamboat one time all the way down the Mississippi from St. Paul, Minnesota to New Orleans. She had a story about every place they'd been and described a lot of food I don't think I would have tried, but it did sound interesting.

She asked if I had read *Tom Sawyer* yet and I told her

it hadn't been in any of the classroom libraries I'd encountered so far. "Oh, my," she told me. "You're in for a treat." She went on to say that Mr. Jenkins had been a big fan of Mark Twain. I was pretty sure I had heard of him before.

"I would say for Mr. Jenkins the high spot of that whole steamboat ride was the stop in Hannibal," Miss Lydia told me. "The house Mark Twain grew up in is a museum now, you see, and for Mr. Jenkins it was like stepping inside the pages of his favorite book. There was the tree outside the bedroom window that Mr. Twain and Tom Sawyer both used when they snuck out of the house. There was Becky Thatcher's house, just down the street a piece. We even went into Injun Joe's cave. It was wet and cold and it gave me the shivers but good."

I didn't know if she was talking about real people or made-up characters or both, but it made me want to get my hands on that book.

She told me how they got to New Orleans just in time for Mardi Gras, a celebration that kicks off Lent and sounds like a cross between Cinderella's ball and a Halloween party for grown-ups. She showed me a little mask covered in peacock feathers that was so old the elastic crumbled when she tried to put it on. So she held it up to her face and told me, "Every day for a week there were parades and costumes and banquet tables loaded with oysters and crawfish and shrimp and, oh my, it makes my mouth water just to remember. Every night there was another ball with dancing and champagne and even more food. We were completely tuckered out, Mr. Jenkins and I, coming back on the train, but it made for a lifetime of memories. It did that."

She told me about sleeping in a Pullman car on a Santa Fe Railroad train and how the wheels on the track clickety-clacked in a rhythm and the coach swayed so that it was like being rocked to sleep. The way she described it was almost poetic. I'd never heard such beautiful words coming from someone unless they were reading from a book.

I asked why they stopped traveling and she didn't answer, but such a dark cloud came over her face I changed the subject.

I found out you can learn a lot about history from an old person if you listen. And Miss Lydia could sweep you up into a story so that you could almost see and smell and taste the things she described. It was a lot more interesting than any schooling I'd had.

I told her that and asked if she'd ever thought about teaching. She looked tired all of a sudden and said that her father hadn't believed in educating girls, that he considered it begging the devil for trouble.

I said, "Yeah, I asked Daddy one time what he

thought my chances were for getting into college and he said 'slim and none.' I thought at first he meant I wasn't smart enough, but then he told me he wasn't gonna throw hard-earned money into the wind when he knew good and well I'd be married and changing diapers before I was twenty."

Miss Lydia sat with her head down, quiet for so long I thought she had dropped off to sleep. My Grandma Wharton did that, her last few years. Talking along, she'd ask you a question and, before you could finish your answer, she'd be snoring.

But Miss Lydia raised her head and looked me in the eye. "I expect you know I think your daddy has more sense than most of what passes for men in this town." I nodded and she went on without blinking. "Well, that's not necessarily sayin' much."

I needed to chew on that a while and Miss Lydia used the time to study her hands in her lap. Then she let out a big breath and said, "Billie Marie, you got rules to follow while you're living under your parents' roof and that's good and that's important. But the fact of the matter is, you're not gonna always live under your folks' roof and nobody in this world has got a right to tell you what you are or aren't gonna do with your life. And the only person who can figure out what you're capable of is you."

Well. That was a lot bigger picture of my life than I'd

ever seen. I closed my eyes to look at it and she went on.

"I'm not sayin' you got to decide right this second what you want to be when you grow up. I'm just sayin' you don't have to give up the right to make that decision to your daddy or anybody else."

I nodded. I couldn't think of anything to say, then or for most of the afternoon. We could work together by then without talking, though, and the air wasn't thick like when Mama was mad. I had so much in my head I couldn't have formed a whole sentence that made sense anyway. That night in my room I went another round with the hand mirror, wondering just who that was looking back.

The next day the sun was shining, and Miss Lydia was nearly as giddy about it as I was. It had been wet and gray for so long we'd gotten used to it and almost forgotten what pretty weather was like. I spent the morning trying to make sense of the spindly plants sticking up out of the mud in our garden and at lunch Miss Lydia and I sat on the cistern outside her back door with our plates in our laps and our glasses of tea beside us.

When she had finished, she leaned back on her elbows and squinted at the sky. "This is the kind of day I'd order for St. Swithin's, wouldn't you?" she said.

"Who?" I thought us Catholics pretty much had the market cornered as far as saints go, but that was one I'd never heard of.

Miss Lydia closed her eyes and recited, "St. Swithin's Day, if it does rain, full forty days it will remain. St. Swithin's Day, if it be fair, for forty days t'will rain no more." She looked at me. "You never heard that?"

I shook my head. "But when is it, Miss Lydia? And what will we do if it does rain that day?" I was looking out over a sea of mud in her garden and the story of Noah was still fresh in my memory.

She chuckled and put her hand on top of my head. I could feel the warmth in my hair as it pressed against my scalp. "Well, now, it's straight-up middle of July, but don't go getting superstitious on me. It doesn't mean a thing, any more than Friday the thirteenth. Anything bad ever happen to you just because the thirteenth of a month fell on a Friday?"

I said, "Nooo." But I was thinking that didn't mean nothing ever would. Laughing at superstitions was the same as inviting bad luck in my book.

After lunch we agreed we couldn't bear to be cooped up inside, so we worked in her flower garden that afternoon pulling weeds and spent blossoms. Her brogans kept getting sucked into the mud and she finally slogged over to the back step and took off her shoes and stockings. I'd never seen an old person go barefoot before.

She caught me humming and asked what the tune was. It was just an old jump-rope rhyme, but she insisted

I say it out for her. She liked it so much she made me say it again. The third time through she chimed in.

It was downright funny—her chanting, "Cinderella, dressed in yellow, went upstairs to kiss her fella." She was so serious, like it was really important to get it right. Then she asked if I knew any more. Boy, did I.

She was a fast learner. Like she'd said when she talked about the levee breaking—she had a better memory than most. And she just loved "A my name is Alice." We went back and forth taking turns with the letters and, without talking about it, started competing to see who could come up with the strangest stuff.

Several times we had to take a giggle break before we could get more words out, like after her "P my name is Pocahontas and I'm gonna marry a Potentate. We're gonna live in Pooterville and sell Pumpkin hammers." We both very nearly had to change our pants.

Saying out jump-rope rhymes like that, laughing so hard, both of us barefoot—it was just me and my friend that day. All the years between us melted in that bright sunshine.

Our days had turned into a routine. I'd sleep late, do the supper dishes from the night before, then clean house like a whirlwind with the time I had left. A few minutes before noon I'd walk up to the post office and be grunted at by Lewis McEntire, drop our mail off at home and take Miss Lydia hers.

There could have been a tunnel between the post office, Miss Lydia's house, and ours for all else that existed those weeks. Never a movement, any sign of life, never a sound except when Curtis drove by or my folks came home at night. I didn't hear them leave in the morning and they were a couple of dirty zombies when they dragged in. Sometimes I was already asleep and didn't hear them then. I'd count the dirty plates in the sink the next morning to convince myself they'd been there at all.

Miss Lydia would always have a big meal ready and while we ate we'd talk like we hadn't seen each other in months. After the dishes were done, I never knew what was in store.

One day she taught me how to make piecrust and biscuits. When the flour finally settled we both looked like ghosts.

Another day she asked if I knew how to crochet, and I shook my head. "Your mama can, can't she?" she asked. I got the impression Mama was going to lose a lot of points in Miss Lydia's book if I said no.

I answered, "Yeah, she can. But I'm left-handed and she had to give up the one time she tried to show me. She said it was hopeless." I shrugged.

Miss Lydia stared off into the distance so long I started wondering where she'd gone. Finally she nodded like she'd been listening to somebody. She tilted her head toward a big upholstered footstool and said, "Bring that over here." It was a minute before I was sure she was talking to me.

"Put it right there." She motioned in front of her chair. When I had moved the big beast she leaned forward and patted it, meaning I should sit, while she reached her other hand into the needlework bag on the floor to her side.

She handed me a ball of yarn and a crochet hook and got one of each for herself, then said, "Just pretend I'm in the mirror and do everything I do."

I didn't start out with very high hopes, but in an hour's time I learned how to make a chain and come back across it in single-crochet stitches. I thought she was pretty smart and told her so.

She bah-humbugged me. "No hill's too big for a climber," she said, but you could tell she was pleased.

No matter what else we did, we worked on crocheting a little bit every afternoon after that. On days I helped her, she gave me a dollar when I left. I'd saved up about twelve dollars in three weeks' time. Whether it was a work day or not, I took her garbage out last thing. I figured I could at least ease her aggravation with Curtis that small way.

Then I'd make supper and eat in front of the TV, and reheat everything when Mama and Daddy came in after dark. Once in a while I thought about waiting to eat with them, but it seemed like they were too tired even to talk to one another—and it wasn't like they complained for lack of my company.

I wondered how it was going with the levees, but didn't think I should bring it up in case they'd managed to forget for a few minutes. After talking to Miss Lydia all afternoon I didn't mind being quiet anyway.

One rainy day, Miss Lydia brought out some old picture albums and went through them naming everyone. She had been the youngest of four, the only girl, and had grown up in Sedalia. All news to me.

Sedalia was home to the state fair and I'd only been there once, so it seemed like a big deal to me. That was funny to her for some reason. I asked about her brothers and her voice caught when she told me, "They're gone. All of 'em. Joe went last, eight years ago. The year before I lost Mr. Jenkins."

I had been beating myself up because I just barely remembered Mr. Jenkins going between the car and house a few times. But if he had died when I was four, I was probably in the clear. I asked what he was like, then wondered if I should have. Speaking up still felt strange.

Miss Lydia turned the page and tapped a picture. It was an old-fashioned brown-tone photo of a bride and groom, the same kind I'd seen in other old albums. The man is always sitting and the woman stands next to him, her hand on his shoulder and maybe a broom up her behind, stiff as she looks. The clothes in this one looked fancy and expensive.

I stared at the woman's face and pretty soon Miss Lydia showed up in there. It was definitely her eyes and eyebrows, her nose—the only thing different was no wrinkles or smile. These days she looked like she was smiling even when she wasn't—that was how her face had settled into old age.

She had been really pretty and, when I glanced back up at the real thing beside me on the horsehair sofa, I realized she still was. You just don't think about an old person being pretty, but there it was.

I studied Mr. Jenkins but couldn't tell much except his eyes looked honest and he grew a whopper of a mustache. I looked back to Miss Lydia and waited.

"Avery," she said. There was so much just in the way she said his name. The connection between her eyes and the picture on the page seemed as real as something I could touch. Then it faded like smoke as she came back to the present day.

"He was a good man," she said. I told her I could tell and her smile got bigger. "If you ever decide to get married, I hope it's because you've found a man as fine as my Avery."

If? *If* I decided to get married? The only women I

knew who had never married were either butt ugly or leaning heavily toward crazy. Staying single hadn't exactly been a choice.

I couldn't imagine why on earth I wouldn't want to get married. So I could stand behind the counter at Penney's the rest of my life? I wasn't going to college, so I couldn't teach school. And there wasn't much else for girls like me.

It's not like I didn't know there were extraordinary women out there who had done amazing things. But that was just it. As far as ordinary women went, the kind who were born in the middle of nowhere to dirt farmers— those women got married if they could and then had babies if they could. That was their dream. I had never heard it talked about as a choice.

My brain was getting more of a workout than it ever had at home or in school. I began to wonder if those places were mainly teaching me not to think.

Miss Lydia turned the album page without saying more and several pictures of two little girls had me wondering if she had had daughters who didn't get to grow up. But you don't blurt out that kind of question. Not when somebody's eyes look like hers did then.

It turned out the pictures weren't in order. These were of Miss Lydia herself and her friend Lucy. She and Lucy had been closer than most sisters, she told me. I had always wished for a sister to talk to and it was news to me you could be even closer to a friend.

Miss Lydia said, "Pneumonia took her in 1901," in such a matter-of-fact voice I wasn't sure if I had asked out loud. "Such a shame. Anymore, a couple of days' bed rest and a prescription and she and I would have been back out in the haymow playing."

She needed so badly to clear her throat. I didn't know what I'd do if she broke down. But then she took a sip of tea and asked me to tell her about my friends.

I said, "Oh, I don't really have any." But that sounded so pathetic coming out I added, "Not yet, anyway."

"Don't have any friends!" Miss Lydia was astonished. "Why ever not?"

"Well, there's only two other girls in my grade at school and they've been best friends since before I met them." It was a fact so old I didn't have to consider it. It's just how it was.

But Miss Lydia did. "You're tellin' me they neither one have room for two friends?"

The idea of Karen and Debbie being friendly toward me was laughable. Making fun of me was part of the glue that stuck those two together and kept them feeling superior in their one little foot of space on the planet. I covered my smile with one hand and said, "Nope."

"Well, then, what about the girls younger or older?" she said.

"No." I shook my head. "Nobody has friends outside their own grade. It's almost like a rule."

"Why, I never heard the like!" she sputtered. "The very idea that a year or two is so sacred." It did seem silly when you put it that way.

"Just the way it is." I had never questioned it so I couldn't explain it.

"Well, what about the boys in your class? Any makin's of a friend there?"

That was so outlandish I started giggling.

"Oh, never mind," Miss Lydia sighed. "If the very idea sets you off, you're likely past the age when you could have had a boy for a friend." I was pretty sure what she meant, but made a mental note to roll that comment around some when I was alone.

Then she harrumphed. "Make me a promise, Billie Marie. I want you, when school starts up again, to take a real hard look in the classes up and down a year. See if you can't find somebody you can be friendly to."

"I can't do that!" The very idea made me itch. I'd gotten pretty used to being invisible at school, too.

"I don't see why not." When she looked me in the eye like that it was impossible to look away. "Why, I'm . . .

pretty near sixty-five years older than you and we're friends, aren't we?"

I hadn't been so surprised since the day the town disappeared and Miss Lydia yelled out my name. But I sure liked her. If she thought we were friends, I guessed we were.

That night I crocheted her a potholder that was only a little bit crooked, and the next day she told me it was the prettiest thing she'd ever seen.

Chapter Four

Almost five weeks had gone by, all told, before the day it all happened. St. Swithin's Day, straight-up middle of July, dawned sunny and bright and, even if I couldn't plan on confiding it to Miss Lydia, I felt a wave of relief. Middle of the morning, I was out back trying to pick enough straggly green beans for that night's supper when Curtis drove his pickup into the alley from the back way. He yelled to get my attention and then said, "Come on, get in and go to town with me."

"No, thanks," is all I said.

Then he held up some money and a piece of note-book paper. "Mom wants you to get her some groceries." That oily-looking smile again. "Guess she don't trust me with woman's work."

I could hardly believe Miss Lydia would make me go anywhere with Curtis. I stepped out into the alley so I could see past our garage and across the street. Just then

Miss Lydia straightened up from her flowers and waved. She could see Curtis's truck right there plain as day, so I thought she was saying to go on.

I still didn't want to. But I figured that's part of what friends are for, to do things for you they don't want to do. Just because you're their friend.

After I got in, Curtis backed out of the alley instead of pulling on through. It was an odd thing to do, but I was trying not to think too much about where I was. Much later I remembered being barefoot, which right there would have made a sashay into the IGA out of the question.

I tried to run when he pulled up to the back of the school and stopped. I swear I did. I've imagined it a million times the last five years and every single time I get away somehow at that instant and run for home.

Sometimes I bite his hand and he lets go. Sometimes I kick him where it hurts and make off while he's bent double. Sometimes I just scream and it surprises him so, he lets go. Just for a second. Just long enough.

A second would have changed my life and everything in it since. But the truth is, he grabbed my arm and dragged me out the driver's door and over to the building before I could even get my feet under me. He held on so tight while he broke a window next to the handle on the big double door I got burns on my wrist. Deep enough to scar just a little. I still wear a purple bracelet of skin when it turns bitter cold.

But I forgot about my wrist hurting when the back of my head hit the lunchroom floor. For a few seconds I thought I was going to pass out, but I guess adrenaline kept me awake.

I slapped and kicked and clawed best as I could until Curtis backhanded me across the face so hard I saw stars. I quit trying to hurt him then. But I couldn't stop trying to get away.

The sun was shining straight at me through the bare windows and I squeezed my eyes shut against the glare. I tried to block out everything else, too, but couldn't. Behind the blood red of my eyelids, I couldn't stop feeling or tasting or hearing or smelling.

I knew it was Curtis's tongue shoving into my mouth, but it felt like a snake trying to muscle its way past my teeth and it tasted like a dirty ashtray rinsed in coffee.

His whiskers scraped my cheeks like sandpaper, and the smell of Brylcreem in his hair mixed with stale sweat on his clothes and the smell of a million school lunches.

He started grunting while he pulled at my clothes. It sounded like a hog going after his mealtime slop. Sometimes now I imagine I threw up on him and it disgusted him so he let me go. But no matter how many times I gagged with his mouth mashed against mine, nothing came up. My stomach was empty. Sometimes I wonder if eating breakfast that day might have saved everything.

Finally, Curtis took his mouth off mine so he could threaten to kill me if I didn't stop struggling. And then came a pain like I didn't know existed. White-hot pain like a thousand fingernails scraping my insides out. So bad I thought it couldn't get any worse.

But it could and it did, again and again, until the pain swallowed me up and that's what I became. I couldn't separate it from anything else in my being. Lightning bolts hit with the rhythm of waves on a beach, one following another. Each one tearing me open, ripping me apart.

And sometime during this Curtis grew strangely calm. He cooed at me, droning on like he was in a trance. Like he was trying to lullaby me to sleep. "That's it. Idn't that good? Idn't that what you wanted?"

And somehow, from somewhere behind his voice in my ear and beyond the pain I had become, I heard the sound of someone crying.

It must have been me.

Chapter Five

Curtis had roared off in his truck and I had run all the way home before I realized the house key had fallen out of my pocket somewhere. I'd been sitting on our back step less than a minute before Miss Lydia was right there. She must have been watching for me.

She sat down trying to comfort me and at the same time ask questions I just couldn't answer. I kept shaking my head and wincing away from being touched. I wasn't sure I'd ever be able to untangle the words in my head and string them together in a way that made sense.

But then she saw the blood running down my legs and she started crying too. That made me feel even worse. I'd never, ever be able to pretend it hadn't happened now, because it didn't belong to just me anymore. She knew and there was no way she could ever not know again.

She stood up and tried to get me to go with her. She wanted to take me home. To her house. That house.

Where he lived too. I tried to tell her no but couldn't get anything out beyond, "What if he . . . what if he . . ."

Miss Lydia stopped crying just enough to say, "Oh, he knows enough not to show his face." Then she led me across the street by the hand like nobody had done since I was four years old.

She took me upstairs and started to run water in the bathtub, but the hairs on the back of my neck stood up when I thought about taking off my clothes. I couldn't and I told her so.

She left and came back with two big old terrycloth bathrobes and told me if I'd take a bath, she'd put one on too.

I didn't want anyone to see me naked and told her so, and she said to put my clothes outside the door. She'd wait. I heard her crying even with the door closed. It was a terrible sound.

I'd only heard an old person cry once before. My guess is, heartbreak just comes as less and less a surprise as your life goes on. But I'd heard my grandma cry after they found my Uncle Junior under his tractor, and it was just the way Miss Lydia was carrying on now.

When I lowered myself into the tub, the hot water scalded the raw place between my legs, but it also told me my muscles had been tied in knots for so long they were starting to ache. I scrunched down until my chin was touching the water's surface. Tried to let my arms and legs float.

The water was soon pink with the sticky blood soaking off me and I grabbed for the soap and washcloth. I scrubbed every inch I could reach, but rinsing off with that pink water—washing myself in my own blood— made me feel like I'd never be clean again.

Later, Miss Lydia and I sat together on her couch downstairs in those ratty old robes while my clothes went through the washer and dryer. She petted my hair when I laid my head in her lap.

It was easier to talk, not looking at her. So I told her about the day Curtis came to our house and how I had been scared of him then. "I guess I should've told you," I said. "I just had no idea . . ." I felt so stupid.

She started trembling and her voice came out shaky. "Oh, honey. Oh, honey, I didn't know. I just didn't know or I would've done anything in the world to stop him." Then she said she was sorry, that she never should have had a son in the first place. I knew that wasn't right and tried to tell her so.

That made her cry more, but after three false starts she told me. "I wasn't much older than you," she said, "when my own daddy . . . oh, child. My own daddy hurt me like that. He did. He did."

A jolt shot through me like a zap of electricity and I

whipped my head around to stare at her. It was her turn to look away. I watched her chin wobble as she stared at the curtained window and forced more words to come out.

"My daddy . . . the one man who was supposed to look after me . . . and he hurt me. Whenever he could get me off somewhere." Her shoulders started shaking, her head dropped to her chest, and tears started dripping down onto my face.

"Oh, Miss Lydia. Oh." There didn't seem to be anything else to say.

"Oh, child, I would do anything to take this away from you. Anything," she said. "I . . . should never have had a child. I never meant to. Because of what he did. What he was. And when I found out I was expecting . . ." She scrunched her eyes tight and spent a minute pulling herself back together. ". . . I prayed to God every night that I was carrying a girl. That there'd be no way to pass it on. And then . . . I had a boy. A boy, a boy, and I felt worse than Typhoid Mary for bringing him into the world."

I felt so bad. Like it was my fault she'd had to remember all that. Like I should have hidden what happened for her sake, not mine.

But the way her face twisted up told me something different: that this was the kind of thing you never forgot, reminded or not. That even if I still owned it, all to myself, there could be no pretending it hadn't happened.

I started wishing I could trade places with Miss Lydia and have all those years between my age and hers over and done with.

And then, all at once, I was tired enough to feel like I could sleep for a few of those years. I was way too tired to think any more.

So Miss Lydia started thinking for me. After my clothes were done and we both got dressed, she said we needed a plan. She said I should stay with her until my folks came home and she'd stick up for me if they said anything about losing my key.

"Are you saying I shouldn't tell them?" I hadn't thought that far ahead yet, but something faint started to claw at my stomach.

Miss Lydia shook her head. "I think it'd be best. Won't undo what's done and you got to remember, I've known your folks longer than you have. Known folks in general longer than that."

I guess she could tell I didn't understand. "My own mama blamed me when she found out . . . well, you know," she said. "And I got a pretty good idea your mama's no smarter than mine was. Your daddy . . . well, your daddy would feel like he had to do *somethin'* about it. And whatever he did, everybody in the countryside would know why sooner or later. And that's just more to talk."

She hung her head and shook it, while tears dripped onto the hands clasped together in her lap. "And . . . honey, the plain, honest truth is that people, most of 'em anyway, are no damned good." She shuddered like she was trying to shake something off. "And there's *nobody* gonna blame you, child, long as I draw a breath."

It sounded like nobody was going to blame Curtis either. The twist in my gut started to feel like fear. I didn't know how I could stand living right across the street. I said, "But . . ." and found I couldn't say his name. I shivered and Miss Lydia pulled an afghan off the back of the sofa onto my shoulders. I shook it off. Tried again. "But he . . ."

"—will never hurt you again as long as he lives," she finished. Then she said, "Trust me."

Well. My mama had told me never to believe anybody who had to tell you to trust them. But I'd had enough doubt planted about Mama's thinking to confuse that issue.

And anyway, I knew she was right about Daddy. And about other people finding out. I'd be better off dead than living in Cumberland if everybody knew.

But I had to trust somebody. This felt a whole lot bigger than me.

❧ 55 ❧

We cooked supper for my folks out of her pantry and she helped me carry it over when we heard them drive in. They tried to yell at me about losing my key, but Miss Lydia interrupted and offered to call Mr. Ripley of "Believe It or Not" on their behalf. She half smiled as she explained that it was the first time she'd met anyone who had never lost anything. The look she leveled at them rendered them both pretty sheepish by the time she was finished. She kissed my cheek before she went home.

I was alone with my parents then, terrified to look them in the eye. Surely they would see I was a completely different person than I had been that morning. They'd want to know why.

But they didn't give me more than the usual glance. Something ominous as a thunderhead was hanging in the air of that little kitchen and they didn't notice.

After my heart slowed down and my hands quit shaking, I asked Mama for permission to take some aspirin. She wanted to know if I had a headache.

I did, from my head hitting the hard wood of the lunchroom floor. But I said, "No, I think I might be coming down with something."

I sniffled a little for effect and a small shock went through me head to toe as I realized this was it. I had decided not to tell.

I had to run to make it to the bathroom before I

threw up. After that I went straight to bed, but a long time passed before I was able to close my eyes, let alone go to sleep.

The sirens woke us up at 3:30. We all jumped out of bed and tried to run out the door at the same time, but Mama made me stay behind. So I stood at our front window and watched the lights on the police cars go around and around, splashing red across my face and onto the walls around me.

Mama came walking home by herself after a while and acted mad that I wasn't in bed. I asked what had happened and she said, "That old fool woman shot Curtis for a prowler when he came draggin' in, like he hadn't done it a million times before. I guess she's gone senile. Now go back to bed."

And I did. But I never did get back to sleep.

Chapter Six

It turned out the river had crested that day. Two days after Curtis's funeral everybody started moving back to town.

Curtis Jenkins's funeral was the strangest I'd ever seen—and I had been hauled to the funeral home more times in my eleven years than I could remember. Around here when anybody dies, everybody goes. I've never figured out whether it's out of respect for the family or out of fear that otherwise, when their own time comes, theirs will be the only body in the room. Probably a little of both.

But this one was different, all right. How do you write a eulogy for a man nobody liked? What do you say to a woman who killed her own son, even when you think it was an accident? The Lutheran preacher just gave kind of a regular sermon. Maybe a little heavy on the "be prepared" theme. In this case it came out sounding a lot more like condemnation than praise for the departed.

The time before and after the service turned into a reunion for all the Cumberland folks who hadn't seen each other since they'd packed and run for the hills. It didn't seem right, all that laughing.

But I don't think Miss Lydia heard a noise anyone made. She just sat in the front pew in her navy-blue dress and black old lady shoes with her hands twisted around a lace-trimmed linen hanky. And she stared straight ahead at nothing. Or at everything, I don't know.

The only time she moved was when I was within reach. I don't know if she could hear me or smell me or what. Without turning her head or blinking she'd reach out, pull me in close, and squeeze until I could barely breathe. I might have wondered if she really had gone around the bend if I hadn't seen just about every kind of behavior imaginable from folks sitting in the front pew of that room that always smelled like carnations.

I remember after Grandma Wharton's visitation Daddy had little red dashes on his white shirtsleeve from Mama's fingernails digging in and drawing blood. Old Man Sullivan stood in front of his wife's casket like a guard dog at her funeral, fairly snarling at anybody who came close. And you never knew whose relatives would get into a shouting match right there over their dead body.

Grief seems to come down to individual style about as much as dancing does.

As for me that day, I had every emotion going on at once. My brain worked so hard it felt like it might seize up. I was horrified and sad and relieved and guilty and still in shock over everything that had happened in just three days' time. The one thought that I kept coming back to was, "Please don't die, old woman. Please live as long as you can, even if you don't want to right now."

It had come to me that if I lost Miss Lydia, I'd be the only person in the whole world who knew what had really happened and why Curtis was in that coffin at the front of the room. And I wasn't sure I could hold all that knowledge inside me without breaking into pieces.

When the trucks rolled into Cumberland and everybody started lugging in the same crap they had lugged out less than a month before, Daddy did feel pretty smart. That presented him a problem. He thought pride was just about the biggest sin you could commit, so now he couldn't say "I told you so" to anybody.

But he must have granted himself special dispensation after the door slammed behind him at home. He'd come in about ready to bust and strut around crowing to Mama about who said this and that and what had he tried to tell all of them a month ago?

And Mama, she'd laugh and egg him on, making him repeat a story he'd just told the day before. It was like they had been in a coal mine or something, dragging home every night dirty and discouraged and too tired to talk. And now they were partners in some kind of secret celebration only the two of them had earned.

It was them and me—a team and a nation of one. I guess it always had been. But now they felt so smart and there was so much they didn't know I couldn't stand to look at them. I could barely be in the same room.

What made the nightmare even worse was that while Daddy came out looking smart, Mama had found a whole new way to be mean. I couldn't believe the things she said about Miss Lydia at our kitchen table and the dirt wasn't even tamped down on Curtis's grave before I heard her make a joke to Missy Hambrick about it being "a heck of a way to cut down on the grocery bill."

This was the old woman who had lived across the street from Mama her entire married life. Her only child was dead, by her own hand. And Mama found it laughable.

I'd always been afraid of her and tried to please her even when I suspected it was impossible. Every time she flew into one of her fits, it'd make me try even harder the next time.

Now I was beginning to suspect there was less to Mama than meets the eye.

One thing I didn't doubt for a second—Miss Lydia had been right when she said, "I got a pretty good idea your mama's no smarter than mine was." Oh, did I thank God every night Miss Lydia had convinced me we were the only ones who needed to know the truth. Then I thanked God she was still alive.

And although I was afraid it was something that would send us both to hell some day, I thanked God that Miss Lydia had made sure there was one thing I'd never have to be afraid of again.

Sure as rain.

Chapter Seven

If the town had been dead for over a month, it was more alive than ever when folks moved back. There were cars and trucks going all day long. Dogs were yapping and kids were yelling and laughing and snotting all over the place. I realized I'd gotten used to the quiet. And I'd liked it.

It was still too wet to get into the fields, so Mama and Daddy were mostly around home the next week or so after the river crested. Mama kept me too busy to think about much of anything other than trying to do things exactly the way she liked. I pretended I still cared.

There was a trip to Milton to restock the pantry. Catching up with the laundry took two whole days with the wringer machine and backyard clothesline. Then there was the slapdash cleaning I'd been doing that Mama now had time to inspect.

We took our meals at the table together for the first

time in months, but those two spent that time yakking at each other like they were still high on the adrenaline that came with Being Right. Either that or they were discussing the separate sections of paper each had their nose buried in. I might have been watching them on TV for all the interaction offered me. Not that I had anything I wanted to say to them.

In the evening after the dishes were done, I'd go to my room and think about Miss Lydia. I hadn't seen her since Curtis's funeral. I knew I ought to go over there but didn't know what I could possibly say. Thank you for killing your son for me? I knew in my heart that's what she had done. Miss Lydia was way too sharp to have mistaken Curtis for a prowler. Even if she had been nervous about her neighbors being gone, like people were thinking.

Over and over I heard her saying, "He'll never, ever hurt you again. Trust me." And that was only a couple of hours after what he had done.

I kept going back over it, trying to figure out the exact moment she had decided what she would do. It seemed important to know—I guess because it still seemed impossible she had done it.

And I kept seeing her sitting in the dark in her nightgown. A shotgun across her lap. Waiting. I wondered, did she cry? Did she pray? Did she ever think "I can't do this" and unload the gun?

I had been over every inch of Miss Lydia's house and I knew where that shotgun lived. It stood barrel-up in the back corner of the coat closet inside the front door. I knew the shells were in the bottom drawer of a kitchen cabinet under the dish towels. I knew she kept the gun unloaded and hid the shells where Curtis would never come across them.

So she had loaded the gun especially for him.

Mirrors can play all kinds of tricks. One of them happens if you stare into one up close until your mind goes blank and your focus goes soft. What you think you see slowly changes until it looks like you're about a hundred years old.

I learned this right around that time. It was an accident, and not a happy one. Because I swear after staring in the mirror for a while it was Miss Lydia's face looking back at me.

That's when I cried for the first time since I'd left her house that day. I cried like I might never stop. I was crying for both of us.

The first day it was dry enough for my folks to go back to the field, I was still in bed when the phone rang a few minutes before noon. I jumped up and answered. It was Miss Lydia, sounding shaky.

"Billie Marie?" she said.

"Uh-huh?"

"Honey, I was wonderin' if you'd go up and get my mail along with your all's and come by for dinner. I've made meat loaf and apple dumplings." Two of my favorites.

I felt as gangly and stupid as I ever had, which was saying something. "Ohhh, Miss Lydia. You didn't need to—"

"Didn't need to. Wanted to." It was almost exactly the conversation we'd had that first day we had become the whole town. I had to smile in spite of my stupid self.

I still wanted to say no, but "okay" is what I heard coming out of my mouth. "Just give me a few seconds to throw some clothes on and brush my teeth—"

"Lord, child—" She interrupted me, then caught herself. "Okay, then, you just come when you're ready."

I wasn't sure I would ever be ready. But I mumbled something she took as a "yes" and hung up.

By the time I'd been grunted at by Lewis McEntire and was heading back home to drop off our mail, I was shaking. It felt a lot like when Miss Lydia first suggested I not tell my parents about Curtis. I was afraid she was going to pretend nothing had happened, and making like everything was puppy dogs and lollipops was more than I thought I could live up to just then. I'd rather stay home by myself.

But just as sure as Curtis had not gone unblamed and

unpunished, Miss Lydia didn't try to make me pretend anything. She had a big smile on her face when she opened the back door but, as soon as our eyes met, her face fairly crumpled in on itself. Then we were in her kitchen hugging each other and bawling.

We rocked back and forth like we were taking turns being the mama and the baby. It was a long time before either of us could say anything that sounded like words.

"What're we gonna do?" I bawled.

Miss Lydia blubbered right back. "Best we can, child. Best we can."

When we finally calmed down enough to let go, we stood at the kitchen sink together and splashed water cold from the faucet onto our faces. Then we shared opposite ends of a tea towel and went to sit down at the table like it was something we had voted on.

Miss Lydia's face was red and blotched as a newborn's. My eyes felt swollen as a toad's. I was self-conscious about making eye contact even though I figured we looked about the same. Or maybe it was because.

"There's dinner, like I said, if you want it." Miss Lydia was as quiet and polite as if I were the preacher's wife. She said, "I don't feel very hungry just yet."

"No, thank you." I felt a little prim myself. "I don't care for anything to eat right now."

She nodded. "Iced tea?"

"I'll get it." I jumped up.

But she was already starting to haul herself out of her chair and I rounded the table just in time to smack into her. It wasn't enough of a collision to hurt either one of us but we did start laughing. She was probably as surprised as I was that spider webs didn't fly out of our mouths, it'd been so long since we'd laughed. We were still smiling when I said, "You sit down there. I know where everything is."

Of course I did and it helped my nerves to get the glasses out of the cabinet where I had put them dozens of times after drying them. To open the right door for the sugar bowl. Go straight to the drawer with the spoons. Have everything feel familiar. My breathing slowed down to normal as I cracked an ice cube tray and started filling glasses.

I was glad to sit down across from her and feel like smiling again but I still had no idea what to say. When she cleared her throat, I sat up at attention.

"How're your folks?" she asked.

"Same as always, I suppose."

I must have looked surprised. "Didn't mean to start anything, child. I was just making conversation," she said. "Your daddy must feel pretty good about stayin' put till the river crested."

"Oh, yeah," I answered. "He's the smartest man he

knows these days." I hadn't meant it to be funny but it was, and we both chuckled.

Thinking about Daddy feeling smart was all it took to remind me what he didn't know. Then it occurred to me that if we *had* moved out of town I'd have been nowhere near Curtis. I felt sick.

"I know," Miss Lydia said and I wasn't sure what I had said out loud. "Believe you me, Billie Marie, I've gone over it a million times. If only your daddy had hightailed it out of here like everybody else . . . if only you weren't helping me out Curtis mightn't have even known you were around, seldom as he was . . . if only if only if only and it doesn't change a thing."

I nodded. "I keep going back to how if I'd just jumped out of the truck, or broken away before he got me inside the schoolhouse . . ." It felt normal to be discussing this out in the open. How strange.

"That sounds a whole lot like blaming yourself and I won't have it." Miss Lydia lifted her chin.

"No, no, no," I corrected her. "I'm not saying it was my fault, I just keep thinking if there'd only been that one second . . ."

"—you could've stopped it? But there wasn't, so you didn't? I tell you, I won't have it!" Her eyes were blazing now.

She was right. I hadn't thought of it as blaming

myself, but by thinking of all the things I might have done and hadn't, it was about the same as saying I caused it. Huh.

"I just wish . . ." I started, but that was the same thought put into different words. It still wasn't right.

"Me, too, honey. I wish a whole lot of things. Me, too." Miss Lydia was staring off somewhere past my shoulder.

"Since we're talking . . ." My heart started pounding. "Can I ask you something?" I took a sip of tea and felt ice cubes chatter against my teeth.

She pulled herself back from wherever she had gone. "Of course you can."

"Are you sorry . . . I mean, have you ever thought since . . . that you wish you hadn't done what you did?"

She looked confused. But to me, there was only one thing to consider. I was wondering how to word an explanation when her face finally settled. She knew what I meant.

"I'm sorry that I had to," she said, as matter-of-fact as she might have been telling me the blackberries were ripe out along her fence.

I felt a terrible churning inside. "But—"

"NO, child. I will tell you as many times as I need to, I am only sorry I had to." Her mouth worked silently for a few seconds. "As for right or wrong? I don't know.

That's for God to sort out, I don't claim to have His judgment. But I am not sorry."

I nodded. She meant it, I knew. Now if I could just figure out how I felt.

Miss Lydia read my face. "But since we're talking, Billie Marie?" She waited until I looked at her. "We always can. I want you to know."

I didn't know what she meant and shook my head.

"We can talk about this. I don't expect it to be fun and it might be painful as hell—"

I was electrified. Now she had brought up God and hell both.

"—and I'm not claiming to know the right answers to anything, but you can ask. Anything. Anytime. I don't want you tryin' to hold this in."

She knew. Of course. She would. We stared at each other. "You understand me?"

I nodded, still held by her eyes.

"Now. Anything else you want to ask me? Or tell me?"

I looked away to think. Finally I said, "We probably ought to start unwrapping your knickknacks and put them back where they belong, don't you think?"

She made a noise like a pressure cooker letting off steam. "Lands, child, you . . ." She shook her head and smiled. "Sure we should. But I think I could eat some meat loaf now, how about you?"

"Yeah, I'm hungry, too." I hadn't realized it until I said it.

"But Billie Marie—"

"I know. I know."

"I *mean* it, honey."

"I know, Miss Lydia. I really do." I spent a few seconds building the next sentence in my head. "And I appreciate that more than I'll probably ever tell you." She smiled. "But I'm having a real hard time sorting this out and right now all I needed to know was were you sorry, and now I do."

She nodded. "As long as you know—"

"I know. I truly do."

"You are not alone."

I just swallowed and nodded.

We worked until about six thirty, then stretched like two cats and called it a day. Miss Lydia went to her bedroom and came back with her purse. Before I could open my mouth she said, "Don't start with me, child," and handed me a dollar.

I understood. This was her way of making some things normal again. And I realized that was exactly what I had done when I suggested we work on her knick-knacks.

I wasn't afraid or mad like before. We weren't pretending everything was the same, we were just hanging onto the things that were. I took the money, gave her a quick hug, and took her garbage with me on my way out.

I was surprised to find Mama at the kitchen stove after I'd banged through the back porch door. I almost blurted out, "What are you doing here?" before I remembered to start weighing my words again. I was home.

"Hi, Mama," I managed.

She turned with the smallest of smiles. "Where've *you* been?" she asked. That might have come off as natural from anybody else. From Mama it sounded suspicious and a little envious, like whatever I'd been up to was probably some kind of forbidden fun.

"Miss Lydia's," I answered. "She cooked din—"

That was all I got out before the tornado blew in. Mama whirled around so fast the wooden spoon in her hand slung spaghetti sauce around two walls. Her face was already red and headed for purple.

"WHAT?" She bellowed. "What in the hell were you thinking? You know I don't want you over there anymore!" She was advancing on me fast.

"Mama, wait!" I said. My head buzzed. "I didn't know anything of the kind, and I—"

She didn't need to hear. "Well, you know now, you little idiot! What are you trying to do—get yourself killed too?"

It wasn't the first time she'd called me an idiot. But it

was the first time it made me mad. Just like that, zero to sixty in about three seconds.

"Now, listen to me for a minute." I fought to sound calm.

"I don't have to listen to you! You listen to me!" she yelled and SWACK! Tomato sauce flew into my left eye as she slapped me hard across the cheek with the bowl of the spoon.

Half my face was on fire. My mind raced and my fingernails dug into my palms. I noticed for the first time that I was tall as her now.

I picked up one of the aluminum-framed chairs at the table and hurled it at the stove as soon as I realized it was in my hands. The sauce pot went flying and a red wave splashed onto the wallpaper and started a wide, gory trail down to the floor. The pot and its lid clattered on the linoleum.

Mama's jaw dropped, but she wasn't speechless long. "What in the hell—," she started.

I picked up the chair left closest to me. I could feel a pulse pounding at my temples, but a strange calm enveloped me at the same time. I was so blind angry with every cell of my being that it all canceled out and left me quiet at the core. Like the eye of a storm.

"Stop cussing at me or this one goes through the window," I told her.

Well. No cartoon character ever looked so wide-eyed with surprise. The way I remember it now I almost laugh, but it was pretty grim then.

Her eyes narrowed and I swear her ears laid back. She fairly hissed at me. "Have you gone completely crazy?"

"Maybe." I was still holding the chair, ready to heave it through the window now just because throwing the first one had felt so good. "It's entirely possible. Look who raised me."

She raised the spoon like she might hit me again. I lifted the chair between us, legs out. Like a lion tamer.

"If you hit me again, you better knock me out." I didn't recognize this person talking. "Because if I'm still conscious, I'll lay you out flat." Whoever she was, she meant it.

A few thick seconds ticked by. Then all the air went out of Mama and her arm went down to her side. She was staring, zombie-eyed, and muttered, "My own child—"

I matched my voice to hers. "—doesn't like being called an idiot?" I wiped at my face and rubbed my eye. "Doesn't enjoy getting hit—and burned, to boot?"

We looked at each other until she blinked. Then I set the chair in its place at the table, turned to go clean myself up, and didn't look back.

My cheek hadn't blistered but even a gentle washing

hurt. When I finished it looked like I had a port-wine birthmark. There was a bloodshot spot toward the corner of my eye but it had stopped stinging. I stared in the mirror acquainting myself with this girl. Then I took a deep breath and headed back to the kitchen.

Mama was exactly where I'd left her. I walked past, got the dishcloth, started wiping sauce off the wall and wringing it back into the pot that still sat on the floor where it had fallen.

"That's ruined, you know." She sounded like a whiny child. I turned to her with a blank face.

I said, "I hadn't planned to eat it. Would you rather I not clean it up?"

Her chin lifted so high I could see up her nose. "No. You made the mess, you can just clean it up yourself." I half expected her to stamp her foot. "And when you're done, you can just cook dinner to replace the one you ruined." She flounced out of the room about as well as a forty-year-old woman can flounce. I went back to wiping and wringing.

When the kitchen was back to square one, I took stock. The chair I'd flung had missed the pot of water boiling for spaghetti. That was a start. I dumped a box of macaroni into it and halfway replaced the lid. Then I turned on the oven and started pulling stuff out of the refrigerator.

Miss Lydia had taught me how to make a white sauce one day and promised it would come in handy. If you can make a white sauce, she'd said, you can make gravy, creamed vegetables, chowders—all sorts of things.

Ten minutes later I had a tuna noodle casserole in the oven and had put some canned peas on to simmer. I mixed up some biscuits and rolled them out on newspaper spread across the table. We didn't need the extra starch with the macaroni, but my parents had never had the biscuits Miss Lydia had taught me how to make and I knew they were a long sight better than Mama's.

It was cooking with a vengeance. That doesn't paint me in the best light, but at the time it seemed as mature as Mama was acting. I could hear the TV blaring and I would have bet she had her nose stuck in a book as well. Whatever it took to tune me out.

Daddy went on and on about how good dinner was. You could almost see Mama's blood pressure rising point by point. When he reached for a third helping of casserole and a fourth biscuit and asked, "Why haven't you ever made it like this before?" she finally spewed.

"I didn't make it. *She* did, after she ruined the dinner *I* made." She jerked her head in my direction.

Daddy studied my face and frowned. He hadn't looked at me since he'd come in. Now he said, "What's that on your cheek?"

"I got burned," I muttered.

"Well, boy, I guess you did!" Good food always made him friendlier. "How on earth did you manage that?"

I counted to four before Mama exploded. "I slapped her smart mouth, that's how!"

Daddy sat with his fork in midair and looked back and forth between us. "Slapped her with what?" he asked, but he was looking at me.

"What was handy," Mama told him. "It just happened to be the spoon I was stirring spaghetti sauce with."

Daddy put down his fork and sat back in his chair, taking in a wider picture. "What did you say to her?" Now he was talking to me but looking at Mama.

"Listen to me a minute," I said.

"Okay."

"No. That's what I said. 'Listen to me a minute.'" It was tattling, sure. But if tattling didn't feel so good people wouldn't do nearly so much of it, and just then I felt like singing it. In three-part harmony, all by myself.

Daddy stared at each of us in turn, then told Mama, "We'll talk about it later." To me he said, "And you, if you're finished, go to your room."

Like I'd had other plans.

Chapter Eight

The next morning I almost jumped out of my skin when I walked into the kitchen and found them sitting in the same chairs. I hadn't seen them both at the breakfast table since winter. There were coffee mugs in front of them and Mama looked like she had either slept too hard or done some serious crying.

Daddy cleared his throat and said, "Sit down, please." I slid into my chair. "Your mother is concerned." Mama kept her head down.

I sneaked a look. He was speaking for her now? He went on. "Don't you think it's . . . well, *unwise* to spend time with an old woman addled enough to take her own boy for a prowler?"

I concentrated on my hands. "Oh, as long as I don't wait till the whole town's been gone a month and then try sneaking into her house at three in the morning, I imagine I'll be safe," I told him.

Mama pounced. "What's wrong with you that you can't spend time with girls your own age, anyway?" she said.

A few weeks earlier I would have winced. "Nothing's wrong with me," I told her. "The only two girls around who are my age live about eight miles away. Plus they're tight as ticks. And even if they did want me in their little club, would you drive me out to their farms all the time?"

She took the bait. "I'm not your taxicab." I had heard that often enough.

"Didn't say you were. Just answering your question."

"I guess what your mother and I don't understand is why. Why do you want to be around an old woman like that?" Daddy looked honestly perplexed.

I didn't mean to, but I started laughing. Then tears sprang to my eyes and I just overflowed all over. I wiped my face on my T-shirt sleeve when I could and said, "She's my friend."

Mama sucked her teeth and shook her head at Daddy like this had proved something.

I concentrated on breathing. It seemed like I could forget to. The eye of the storm was coming back.

I made my face blank. "She talks to me," I said. "She listens to me. She teaches me things. How to cook, how to crochet, how to fix stuff." I took a deep breath. "She likes me."

"Your mother can do all those things with you, can't

she?" Daddy's face was so drawn in on itself it looked like a fist.

"Miss Lydia enjoys it," I said.

"Oh, but—" Daddy started. Then he looked at Mama and whatever he saw stopped him. His eyes came back to me and, for the first time that morning, I remembered the big red splotch on my cheek. I stared at the sugar bowl. From the corner of my eye I saw him study my face.

Several minutes passed with no more said. I got up and slid my chair into place, went to my room and closed the door. I got dressed, then rummaged in the top drawer of my desk for the stationery I'd gotten for Christmas. I took out a piece and wrote in my most careful hand.

> *Dear Miss Lydia,*
> *You can ask me anything and tell me*
> *whatever you want, too. We can talk about*
> *anything under the sun you think needs to be*
> *talked about, as far as I'm concerned. You are*
> *not alone, either.*
>
> > *XOX,*
> > *Love,*
> > *Billie Marie*

I folded it in thirds and slid it into an envelope. I wrote her name on the front, sealed it, and laid it on the sewing machine next to the door so it was ready to grab on my way out. Just then I heard doors slam out in the driveway, one-two, and gravel crunched as the pickup drove away. I opened the door and helped myself to a great big breath of their air.

I thought the two hours doodling with makeup had produced a perfect result. I guess the sun had some harsh thoughts otherwise, though, because Miss Lydia jumped when she opened the door. I was afraid she'd get tangled up in the throw rug and fall. I grabbed her elbow just in case.

"Lands, child," she said. She pulled away like I was something from the circus. "What on earth have you done?"

It's hard to make eye contact with someone who looks horrified at your appearance. I went to the sink and started washing my hands just for something to do. "Mama hit me with the spaghetti spoon."

"Whatever for?" she gasped.

"I tried to tell her something and she didn't want to listen. That's pretty much it."

She was quiet for so long. I finished drying my hands and had no choice but to face her. "This have anything to do with me?" She looked at me so fiercely I couldn't pull my eyes away.

"Oh no, Miss Lydia. Not at all."

She was glaring out from under her eyebrows. "Are you sure?"

"Well, Mama might tell you something different, but as far as I'm concerned this had absolutely nothing to do with you and everything in the world to do with Mama," I told her.

Miss Lydia deliberated a long minute, then nodded. "I made pot roast," she said.

Halfway through the meal she asked, "So underneath all that Cover Girl, what exactly you got goin' on?"

"Some of it may be a bruise by today, but mainly it's a burn."

"You put anything on it besides makeup?"

I shook my head.

She nodded and started telling me about some real-life drama she'd read about in the new *Reader's Digest*.

After the dishes were put away, she told me to go to the big bathroom upstairs and wash my face clean. I didn't want to, but she said something about having seen worse no matter how bad it was. And it did seem silly trying to hide what she knew was there.

When I walked back into the kitchen she got out the poultry shears and cut a big tentacle off a plant in the windowsill above the sink. A clear gel starting oozing out the cut end. When she came at me with some on her fingers, I took a couple of steps backward.

She chuckled. "Aloe vera, Billie Marie. Main ingredient in some of the most expensive skin cream you can buy and that's watered down. Best thing in the world for burns. That's why I keep it in the kitchen."

I winced at her touch. Then I was amazed by how cool the stuff felt as she spread it across my cheek. It looked like it should be sticky, but it wasn't. It was just cool and soothing. I shut my eyes.

"Uh-huh," Miss Lydia agreed. "You take that plant with you when you go, and use some every night and morning until that heals."

"Oh, I can't—" But that's as far as I got. I could see her mind was made up.

Mama was making pot roast when I got home that evening and didn't turn around as I took the plant to my room. I guess Daddy had dropped her off and gone on to run some errand, because the truck pulled in a little later. I heard Daddy tell Mama hello and figured that was dinner call.

He nodded at me without breaking his running commentary about the cultivator breaking down that afternoon. She stood at the stove murmuring at the appropriate junctures.

When she turned, she had filled a plate with food. She grabbed a knife and fork off the table and left the room without a word. A minute later we heard the TV come on. Daddy and I looked at each other. He shrugged and made a plate from the pots on the stove and then sat down at the table with the morning's newspaper.

I weighed options while I filled my own plate. Then, carrying it in one hand and a glass of water in the other, I left Daddy with the paper and walked to the living room. Mama wasn't so much watching TV as glaring at it. I kept on walking and ate my dinner behind my closed bedroom door.

And that's how we ate from then on, in three separate rooms, no tie left to tether us to the kitchen table.

As I passed through the living room with my empty plate after that first silent dinner, the phone rang. Mama's expression didn't register any change, so I went over and grabbed it on the second ring.

"Thank you." It was Miss Lydia. It took me a minute to remember the note I had slipped in with her mail.

"Sure. I meant it."

"I know you did, Billie Marie, and I thank you. Now, is your mama there?"

I nearly choked. "Oh, no—well, I mean yeah, but—" Talk about a disaster just waiting to happen.

Miss Lydia chuckled and said, "Oh, lands, child, don't worry. I got some business with her that's got nothin' to do with you."

"Mama?" I had to say it three times before she pulled

her eyes away from the screen and frowned at me. "It's for you."

"Who is it?"

"Miss Lydia," I said and, when that news registered, she looked downright scared. I had to move for her to get to the phone, and I took the opportunity of being on my feet to get out of Dodge.

I took my plate to the kitchen and washed it. Then I washed it again. I was very, very thorough.

Mama leaned against the kitchen doorjamb a couple of minutes later. "I never would've dreamed," she said to Daddy.

"Hmmm?" He was still glued to the paper.

"It was Lydia Jenkins." That got his attention. "She doesn't have anybody to take her to town now that Curtis is . . . gone, and she asked if I would."

"When?" Daddy frowned.

"From now on, I guess." The two of them stared at one other like they'd just dug up a body in the backyard and were each trying to decide if the other had put it there.

Chapter Nine

*T*he next day I waited for Miss Lydia to tell me about
her conversation with Mama, but we passed the midday
meal chitchatting about nothing in particular. We were
washing dishes before she got serious, and then the subject wasn't what I'd expected.

"Billie Marie?" she said. "We've agreed we can talk
about anything needs to be talked about, haven't we?"

Of course we had. "Uh-huh, sure."

"Then I have to ask. Have you started getting your
monthlies yet?" She was staring out the window at her
garden.

My first thought was magazine subscriptions. Why
would she ask about that? I hadn't subscribed to anything
since *Highlights* when I was a little goober. Then, ohhh.
Of course. I shook my head. "No, not yet. Why?"

"Your mother *has* told you where babies come from,
hasn't she?" Her voice shook a little.

"Well, yeah," I said, remembering that awful morning with Mama all red-faced and stammering, getting mad at me because she had to talk about it at all. "Sort of."

Miss Lydia took me by the shoulders. "No 'sort of' about it, child. Either she did or she didn't."

I could feel a pulse in my ears, pounding out a warning. "Well, she told me about the egg and how if it's not fertilized, the stuff gets passed once a month and what to do . . ."

"Billie Marie." I'd never seen Miss Lydia so sober. "Did she tell you *how* the egg gets fertilized?"

"Well, no, but—" But all of a sudden I did know. And then there was a freight train inside my head and I saw a big dark spot like I'd stared too long at the sun and, as my knees buckled, I was thinking *oh-my-god-oh-my-god-oh-my-god-the-joke-that-man-that-comment-that-look-this-is-what-they-meant-but-Mama-and-Daddy-and-Miss-Lydia-and-Mister-Jenkins-and-oh-my-God-oh-my-God-everybody-who-has-ever-had-a-baby-that-awful-that-awful-it-wasn't-just-it-wasn't-just-Miss-Lydia's-father-and-then-Curtis-inherited-this-terrible-idea.*

Miss Lydia's face was only a couple of inches from mine when I opened my eyes and I could see myself reflected in her glasses, scared and small, same as I felt. When I realized I was on the floor, I raised up so fast we banged heads and bounced apart like a couple of stooges, but neither of us laughed.

She steadied herself against the counter while I got

my feet under me. I spoke first. "Do you think . . . I mean, are you saying . . . oh, Miss Lydia, do I have a baby inside me now?"

It sounded ridiculous out loud. Mama didn't even let me wear a training bra yet, even though I needed one. It hadn't been that long since I'd packed away all my Barbie stuff.

If I had a baby in me—it came all at once—then everybody would find out. I had to lay my cheek against the cool Formica counter in front of me.

"Aw now, child," Miss Lydia started. I heard it catch in her throat. Calling me "child." She was trying to stay calm, but her hands were shaking a lot worse than usual. "I seriously doubt it. I really, really do. But I had to ask. . . ."

I had a jumble in my head and was trying to fit the pieces together. "But . . . if I haven't gotten the curse yet, is it possible?"

"Billie Marie! It's hardly a curse!"

"Well, that's what Mama calls it," I said.

Miss Lydia shook her head like she felt sorry. "Well, you call it whatever you want, but that mama of yours is somethin' else."

But she wasn't thinking about Mama. It looked more like she was trying to remember the combination to a safe she hadn't opened in years. She blew out a lungful of exasperation.

"I don't know." She was matter-of-fact, like I had

asked if we were going to have a white Christmas that year. "It doesn't seem like it would work that way, but I just don't know. It's a whole lot easier to find out you're not expecting early on than if you are."

"So what do I do?" My chin started quivering. I couldn't make it stop.

"Lemme think on it."

I had an inspiration. "Is there something I can do, something I can take, I mean, to make sure it doesn't, didn't, happen?"

"NO!" Miss Lydia started out of her chair and I jumped. "Oh, lord, no, child, no. Don't you even begin to think about hurting your body in any way, shape, or form. Just put that outta your mind this instant."

"I just thought ... maybe there was some easy way. . . ." Just thought. Just wished. Just hoped. Just make it go away.

Miss Lydia's mouth twisted up like she'd bitten into something sour. "If there was, wouldn't anybody have a baby they hadn't planned on, now, would they?"

Oh. Of course. That girl who went away to take care of a sick aunt for six months. The other one who gave birth to a nine-pound "preemie" seven months after her wedding. All the women who were married up all nice and tidy and still liked their kids about as much as canker sores.

"So what do I do now? Just wait to see if my stomach starts growing?" I felt light-headed.

Miss Lydia shook her head. She looked a little cross. "I said, 'lemme think on it.'" I didn't see how I was going to think about anything else until I knew for sure.

I sat up straight as a yardstick and gasped. "I fainted!"

"Yeah?" She frowned.

"Well, on TV, that's always the first sign somebody's going to have a baby. That's how you know." I felt cold.

Miss Lydia smiled for the first time since the subject had come up. "Well, now, honey, that's TV. You just can't believe everything you see on it. Besides, that's men writin' about woman things for you."

Oh. I had no problem with the difference between fact and fiction, but I'd always thought even fiction was based on something true. I hadn't thought about anybody just plain getting it wrong.

Miss Lydia interrupted my thoughts. "I probably shouldn't've even brought it up. Chances are . . ."

"Now, wait a minute," I said. "Of course you should've brought it up if it was on your mind. That was our deal, remember?"

Miss Lydia smiled, but there wasn't a shred of happiness behind it. "That it was. Just promise me you'll try not to worry yourself sick over it, will you? What's done is done and worrying about it won't change a thing about what is and what isn't."

I nodded and swallowed what was rising in my throat.

Chapter Ten

Time has a frustrating way of continuing on at the same rate no matter how many terrible things have happened. So one day just kept dragging on after another. Each one with an equally anxious yesterday and tomorrow for bookends. I ate and slept and went to Miss Lydia's. I tried not to bring it up in case she'd put her worries aside. I tried to push on my stomach only when nobody was around to see it.

After a while, I'd forget to be afraid for stretches of two or three hours. Then I'd remember and feel guilty, like I had changed my fate just by letting my guard down. It's hard to talk yourself out of stupid thoughts when you're scared.

And I had plenty of stupid thoughts to spread around. For one thing, just the idea of Mama and Miss Lydia in the same car made me break out in an itch. I couldn't see Mama leaving her usual behavior at home any more than I could see Miss Lydia putting up with it and couldn't imagine how that was going to average out. Of course I was rooting for Miss Lydia, but I did still have to share a roof with Mama. If they were going into Milton together, I was ready to be the go-between, if not the referee.

That Saturday morning I walked into Mama's bedroom and was surprised to see her dressing up like she was going to church. Once she was on the winning end of the zipper in back of her dress, I said, "You want me to go with you?"

She jumped like she hadn't known anybody was there. She's so skittish. "No. Why would I?" She stood in front of the vanity while she brushed her hair back.

I wasn't sure how I felt about being left behind. I watched out the front window when Miss Lydia hobbled out and dumped herself into our car. I couldn't stop watching until long after they were out of sight. Then I turned on the TV and sat watching cartoons. Pushed on my stomach every couple minutes to see if anything was going on there.

Daddy usually ate at the grain elevator when Mama was gone to town so I was surprised when I heard his truck in the driveway at straight-up noon. I had the TV off and was in the kitchen before the back screen-door slammed. By the time he came in, I was pulling cold cuts and sliced cheese out of the refrigerator.

"Aw, now," Daddy said as he passed, "Don't go to any

trouble. I can make a sandwich for myself."

As food preparation goes, I'd never seen Daddy do more than butter his own bread. But now that I thought about it, making lunch for just the two of us would be pretty strange. Kind of like I was taking Mama's place. Cooking for all three of us never felt like stepping into somebody else's role.

It seemed like the rules were changing every day. Either that, or becoming visible was making me pay more attention.

I got out plates and started building a ham and cheese sandwich on Wonder Bread. When Daddy came back from washing up I couldn't think of anything to say, so I kept my head down with my hair hiding my face.

Once he started slathering on the mayonnaise, though, another dilemma stuck a horn in my gut. With Mama gone, where did we eat? I took my time getting ice and let the tap run a good long while. I waited.

When I turned, he was sitting at his usual spot, but the newspaper was nowhere to be seen. I caught his eye without meaning to and his face was a big question mark. I froze.

"Something wrong?" he asked.

"Uh . . . uh-uh. Why?"

"I dunno. You look like you just came across a fresh train wreck."

I could hardly leave then. I sat down in the chair that

used to be mine when we all ate together.

Everything was off balance. It felt like the table was going to tip and slide everything on it crashing down into Mama's empty chair. I said, "No . . . I just remembered something."

"What?"

"What what?" It sounded like a smart remark. I wanted it back as soon as I said it.

"What did you just remember?"

"Nothing." My face was on fire. This was my father. And I was just as relaxed as I would be if somebody plunked me down to lunch with the president.

He sat and chewed, trying to read me. "How's your cheek?"

"Oh, the old 'does your face hurt? It's killing me'?" I listened to my nervous laugh like it was coming from some other stupid person.

Daddy didn't smile. In fact, he frowned a little. "No, I wanted to know. How's your cheek?"

I coughed and cleared my throat. "It's okay. Miss Lydia gave me this plant stuff to put on it, and it started healing really fast."

"Plant stuff?"

"Yeah, hollow vera, I think she calls it. It's this plant that has goop inside the leaves and it's the best burn medicine there is, she says."

He nodded. "You really do enjoy spending time with that old woman, don't you?"

I was surprised. "Well, yeah," I told him. "I mean, she's interesting and funny . . . and she teaches me all kinds of stuff . . . and it's way better than——." My face heated up again.

He let it go. But after a minute passed he said, "How you and your mother getting along these days?"

I would have chosen a whipping over this conversation and it must have shown because, after a few seconds, he nodded as though he'd been answered. He reached for the latest *Missouri Conservationist* on the tea cart by the refrigerator.

I wasn't sure which of us he was letting off the hook, but I was grateful anyway. We finished eating in quiet.

"BILLIE!" Mama yelled. The screen door slammed and I went running. I'd heard often enough that if I intended to eat any of that food I could sure as hell help carry it in and put it away. It took several trips that day just to get everything inside.

"Well!" she said. "That ought to hold us a while!" She was standing with her hands on her hips, surveying the bounty with no little satisfaction. There was color in her cheeks beyond her suntan. She almost looked pretty.

"What's this?" I held up a can of something I didn't recognize.

"Oh. Hearts of palm," Mama said and then laughed. She laughed! "I haven't had those since . . . oh, way before you were born when your father used to take me to the city for dinner and dancing."

He did? I could feel my jaw drop.

"On the way to town Lydia was talking about the old Savoy Grille and it reminded me."

I nodded and put it in the pantry, my head buzzing. Mama dancing? *Daddy* and Mama dancing? There was a picture I couldn't bring into focus. And now Mama was humming!

We finished the chore without talking, but the lack of tension in the room felt like the absence of a third person. Mama hadn't been this lighthearted even when the river crested and she and Daddy were playing Smarter-Than-Thou with the neighbors.

I was crying behind my bedroom door before I had any idea why, but it didn't take long for the hurt to start taking shape. Mama had never had a real friend that I could remember, and now she was starting by taking mine.

I knew deep inside that wanting to keep Miss Lydia all to myself was childish, but I couldn't shake it. It wasn't fair.

Miss Lydia had said we could talk about anything and I was sure ready to take her up on the offer just then. I couldn't go see her without making some excuse, though, and I didn't want Mama to see that I'd been crying. I've seen nature shows on TV and I know what happens when a wounded gazelle gets too close to a lion.

I was going to have to wait to find out what was going on in Miss Lydia's mind, but I couldn't stand back and do nothing in the meantime. She was too important to me. I could at least try to let her know how I felt.

One wastebasket full of crumpled paper later, I settled on a note I could give her.

> *Dear Miss Lydia,*
> *You are my sunshine, my only sunshine.*
> *You make me happy when skies are gray.*
> *You'll never know, dear, how much I love you,*
> *So please don't take my sunshine away.*
> > *XOX,*
> > *Love,*
> > *Billie Marie*

Daddy and Mama yelled their good nights toward my door around 10:30, and I gave it an hour before I peeked out and listened to make sure they were asleep. I held my breath until I nearly passed out before I was sure of Mama's soft sleeping sigh in between Daddy's ripsaw snores.

I tiptoed to avoid the two squeaky boards in the hall-way and let myself out the back door quiet as a cat. Then I lit out for Miss Lydia's like the bogeyman was after me. I slid the pink envelope underneath her front door where she'd see it as soon as she came down the stairs in the morning.

Back out in the street, I heard a dog bark somewhere near the schoolhouse edge of town and it called attention to how quiet the night was. Even though the moon was nearly full and all the streetlights were in a rare state of good repair, there was no movement, no life.

Cumberland looked almost pretty with its edges soft-ened, like a village you might see in a snow globe. I looked at the sky halfway expecting to see a reflection of the town in glass. All I saw was the Big Dipper and about a million other stars. I decided to take a walk.

I love night air in the summertime. The sun takes most of the humidity with it when it goes down and you feel about ten pounds lighter. But it's more than that. Air at night feels different from even the least humid day. It feels promising. Hopeful. Almost electric. Nighttime air feels like a clean slate.

I walked every block. The Sykes family had a dim lamp on in one room, a reminder of their new baby. Elsewise, the houses appeared as uninhabited as they had been the fourth day of June, when I'd had the friendship of a lifetime just waiting for me to come claim it. Before the world had been turned upside down and shaken for the pieces to fall where they might.

When I eased back into my room, I was surprised to see that the clock read 2:35. I caught my reflection in the mirror by the light of the moon and remembered I hadn't worried about what was going on inside me since that morning. I turned side to side to check out my shape before I slid back into bed. Then I lay flat on my back and poked at my middle until I fell asleep. As far as I could tell I wasn't turning into a pumpkin yet.

Chapter Eleven

The phone was ringing when we got home from church the next morning and Mama picked up while I went to change. My unmade bed looked so inviting I decided to lie down for just a minute since I was right there anyway. Next I knew, Mama was shaking my shoulder and asking what was wrong with me.

I said, "I'm tired, that's all," and hoped it was true. I'd watched three pregnant women nod off during Mass just that morning.

"Well, dinner's ready, so come on. That was Lydia on the phone a while ago. She needs you to do something for her after you eat."

"What does she need?"

"She didn't allow and I didn't ask."

I ate in slow motion, still tired and newly filled with dread. The note I'd left for Miss Lydia now seemed more like an accusation than a declaration of affection. I was afraid it had been a terrible error in judgment.

I dragged myself across the street as soon as I'd stashed my plate in the sink. When the back door opened, my eyes filled with tears. "Why, lands, child!" Miss Lydia scooped me up and pressed me against her.

"I'm sorry. I really am," I blubbered.

"Whatever for, Billie Marie?"

I looked at her face and saw that she meant it. "I—I wrote you that note, and—"

Her laugh interrupted. "—and it was just about the sweetest thing I've ever read," she finished.

"But I was afraid you'd think—"

"Come in here." She pointed to a chair and I slung myself into it. She creaked her way into hers and slid something small across the table. It was a ruby the shape of a heart. About the size of a ladybug and set on a jeweler's pin.

"This is for you," she said.

I gasped. "Oh, no, I couldn't—"

"You can and you will." Her chin came up.

"Oh, but now I feel terrible."

"Well, then, you just get over it. Listen to me. *Listen to me.*" I looked up. "How'd your mama act when she got home from town yesterday?"

I looked away and swallowed. "She was smiling and singing like she'd made a new best friend."

"And you felt left out, didn't you?"

I nodded my miserable head.

"Was she harder on you or nicer than usual?" Miss Lydia's eyes were bright. They got like that whenever she latched onto an idea.

"Oh, nicer, for sure," I answered.

She nodded. "And what'd she say about me asking you to come over here today?"

"Nothing. She just said you needed me to do something."

"She didn't say anything about me being senile, or how they oughta send me to St. Joe and put me away?"

My face burned and all I could do was shake my head.

"Honey, look at me."

I didn't want to, but I did.

"When you get to be as old as I am, you can see a whole lot of things you don't necessarily lay eyes on. I've known your mama since she was a kitten and I'd lay money she can't surprise me. Now, say I need somebody to take me to town. If she does that and I pet her till she purrs and it makes your life easier—well, it works out for all three of us, doesn't it?"

I don't know what my face looked like, but it made Miss Lydia laugh. "Don't underestimate old age, Billie Marie. Young people like to think they're smarter, but that doesn't make it so."

I looked down at the pin, bashful to touch it.

She followed my eyes and smiled. "My grandmother gave me that when I was eight and told me to give it to my own girl someday, so that's what I'm doin'."

I felt too much to hold inside and burst into tears.

"Aw, now. Don't cry about it or I'll take it back." I looked up and saw she was joking. "But anytime you even begin to doubt me, you look at that and remember. I love you like my own." She paused. "Better than my own."

We sat there for a long time with a big old cloud of Curtis hanging over our heads. Nothing more needed to be said.

She finally pushed away from the table and reached for the counter. She handed me an envelope. "Before I forget, run this up to the post office and put it through the slot, would you? That way Lewis can send it out first thing in the morning after he figures out he can't read it through the envelope."

"Sure." I glanced at the ruby pin and back to her. She nodded. I picked it up and closed my hand tight. I ran around and gave her a hard, quick hug. "Thank you," I whispered.

She hugged back ferociously. "Thank *you*," she said.

I went home and started on the Sunday dinner dishes. Mama came and leaned in the doorway and asked what

Miss Lydia had wanted. I told her about the letter. She wanted to know who Miss Lydia was writing to that was so important. I said I didn't know, that I hadn't looked.

But of course I had. And I couldn't imagine what business Miss Lydia had with Dr. Vincent Matassa at Riverside Hospital in Kansas City.

Chapter Twelve

The next Saturday I went to town with Mama and Miss Lydia so we could buy me school clothes. I had been afraid Mama would take me on a weekday, shut up in a car with her and nowhere to hide. And once her Lydia glow wore off I knew I could expect her to start building herself back up by chipping away at me.

But instead of sitting beside Mama feeling like I was caught in a steel trap, I sat in the backseat and enjoyed the show.

Miss Lydia gushed, "Why, Miriam, I'd never thought of it that way!" It's likely she really hadn't, either, whatever the topic. That didn't make it a compliment, though, and I knew it. It was fun to listen. Like breaking a code.

"You are *always* thinking, aren't you?" she said.

I nearly burst out laughing at that one. It was like telling the parents of an ugly baby, "Well now, just *look* at that face!" and watching them swell up with pride.

Mama walked into Penney's with her chin up and shoulders back. She had offered to drop Miss Lydia off elsewhere, but Miss Lydia allowed as how she'd like to come along if we didn't mind.

There was one metal folding chair next to the three-way mirror outside the fitting rooms. Miss Lydia settled in there while Mama and I browsed the racks. We loaded up and I headed in to try everything on.

The first outfit I came out in was an orange poorboy sweater and a plaid skirt that even I thought was too short. One look at Mama and I started stammering. "I— I didn't know! I just went by the size, and—." I tried to cover my bare thighs with my hands, then by pulling on the skirt.

"Go change into a decent blouse NOW!" Mama hissed. I was so surprised I turned to the mirror first. The sweater was a narrow tube that stretched to fit and my nipples were about to pop through and say howdy. I crossed one arm across my chest while the other hand still pulled at the skirt. It was the kind of dance you might do if the bishop caught you trying on a bikini.

Miss Lydia called out to the saleslady, "Ida, you've got a tape measure, don't you? Do me a favor and bring it over here." I looked at her. The picture of serenity. Back to Mama. Steam about to come out her ears.

All farm kids know if you whistle at a rabbit running

across the yard he'll stop short and freeze, not even blink, thinking that makes him invisible. I must have rabbit instincts. I was rooted to the spot.

Ida Greene brought the cloth tape and Miss Lydia hoisted herself up with a grunt. She beckoned and I baby-stepped over, every muscle tense. "Arms up," she said and showed me by holding her own straight out to the sides.

She was standing right in front of me good as a shield. I flinched when the tape snaked across my chest.

"Thirty-two-and-a-half," she announced. "'Bout what I figured." She tossed the tape in Ida's direction and said, "Be a big help, would you, and bring us a youth bra, please. Size thirty-two, I'm gonna say *A*."

"Now just hold on a minute!" Mama yelped. That made it Ida's turn to freeze. "She doesn't need a bra! She's only eleven years old!"

Miss Lydia blinked like a cat in a pool of sunshine. "Well, now, Miriam, I don't know as how the need for a bra is measured in years."

"But—" Mama turned bright red. "I didn't wear a bra till I was fourteen!"

"'Course not," Miss Lydia agreed. "You're built like your mama. I believe Billie Marie here favors her Grandma Standish more."

Well. Mama didn't have an answer for that. I took the

opportunity to scoot back into the fitting room. I squirmed out of the plaid skirt and put on one Mama had chosen. Then I wiggled out of the sleeves of the poorboy and stood waiting, arms pinned to my sides.

Presently, a hand came around the curtain offering up a small box. I spent what felt like the next thirty minutes with my arms twisted behind me trying to fasten something unfamiliar that I couldn't see.

"Billie Marie?" Miss Lydia's voice was liquid.

"Huh?"

"Fasten the hook at your waist, in front, then turn the whole thing around and slip your arms through the straps."

Oh. This I accomplished in seconds. Then I slipped back into the sleeves of the sweater and pulled it down around my waist as I stepped out to the mirror. I saw myself at the same time the three women did. Mama and I both gasped.

There are two pictures in my baby album that look like they were taken about four years apart, but the only real difference was one day and a haircut.

The bra and a longer skirt had added about as much age as that haircut.

I wasn't a girl with some extra pudge pushing out her nipples anymore. I had a bustline. Without the camouflage of a loose T-shirt, I had a waist. Because of that narrow waistline, you could see I had hips.

I looked like a woman. Mama, with her narrow hips and nothing much up top, looked like a skinny teenage boy gaping at my reflection in the mirror.

The rest of the day passed in a haze. I vaguely remember trying on outfits and accepting Mama's verdicts. We stopped by Lingerie and she picked up two more bras before we cashed out. By then Mama was convinced it was what she had meant to do all along.

In my mind's eye I kept seeing us standing side by side in the mirror. The same height. Equally astonished.

Chapter Thirteen

⁂

On the way home I was only half listening to Miss Lydia thank Mama a hundred more different ways for hauling her to town until I heard the rhythm of her words change to a halting collection of fits and starts.

"—oh, but I hate to . . . I shouldn't even ask. You've already done so much . . ." she was saying. "I can't . . . expect you . . ." She had my attention then.

Mama was practically shining. "Well, whatever it is, Lydia, you can ask."

"Oh, I hate to," Miss Lydia said. "But I don't know what else to do. I have a bit of bank business in the city that needs tendin' to . . . but, no. I'm not gonna ask you, because I know you're just gettin' back into the fields and you're way behind for the year."

"Mmmm," Mama said. "It *would* be pretty hard for me to get away for a whole day just now."

I thought, *Especially since you've never driven in the City*

*and can't even ride with Daddy without hanging onto the door
handle for dear life.* But I kept quiet and waited to see what
Miss Lydia was up to.

"I know it would, Miriam," Miss Lydia agreed, "and I
can't tell you how much I've appreciated you taking me
to town these past two Saturdays."

"Well, now, it was—" Mama started.

"—and I want you to know I'm not going to take
advantage of your good nature any more after today."

"Oh, but I don't—" Mama tried.

"No, ma'am, I know you'd sacrifice, it's just like you."
I smiled behind my hand in the backseat. Miss Lydia went
on, "but Virginia Simpson stopped by the other day—you
know she's expecting her first—" She waited for Mama
to nod. "—and she was asking if she could do some
cleanin' or sewin' or somethin' for me to make a little
money, and I told her I'd be glad to pay her gas money
and then some to haul me to town when I need to go."

Mama sputtered just a little. "But, Lydia, I never—"

"*No*, ma'am." Miss Lydia set her jaw. "You'd let me
walk all over you, I know you would, it's just the kind of
neighbor you are, good as gold, but I'm not a-gonna do
it."

Mama's eyes sparkled in the rearview mirror.

"No, sir," Miss Lydia went on. "Now, Virginia doesn't
feel up to makin' that long a trip, but I'm not even gonna

ask you about the city, 'cause I know it'd be a hardship and you'd probably do it anyway. I wouldn't mind takin' the train," she said, "but I hate the thought of being up there alone if anything happened. . . ."

I got a glimmer.

"Well," Mama said, "I don't see why Billie can't go with you. Surely the two of you can't cause too much mischief." She took her eyes off the road to flash Miss Lydia a smile.

In that flash, it all made sense. The crafty old bird hadn't thought for a second Mama would take her to Kansas City. But she'd managed to make it Mama's idea to take me.

"Sure! I'll go!" I piped up.

Mama chuckled. "I'll just bet. Lydia, when were you thinking of going?"

Miss Lydia pondered a while. "Well, I might like to go up next Saturday," she said. "But I don't know if these old bones would take the trip twice in one day, so I'd prob'ly have to stay over and come back Sunday."

I was thinking, *Go to the bank on Saturday?* But Mama nodded and said, "Well, I'll have to clear it with James. But since I'm the one who suggested it—and I'll say right now, Billie, you can't go unless you promise to go to Mass Sunday morning—I don't imagine he'll have any objections."

I was so happy I wanted to scream. I had never been away from both my parents a night in my life and the three of us had taken only one trip when I was so little I could barely remember it. Whatever credit Mama wanted to take, let her. I was going on a trip. With my friend.

I could barely stay inside my skin all day Sunday but forced myself to stay home after dinner and act as normal as possible. I didn't trust Mama not to take the trip away if she knew how much I wanted it.

I watched the clock until noon on Monday, then tore across the street like my britches were on fire. I even forgot to stop by the post office until Miss Lydia reminded me later.

She met me with a big shiny smile. "Well, well, my fellow traveler!" she said. I almost bowled her over hugging her.

Then we got down to business. "What would you like to see and do?" she asked. It seemed like such a regular thing to say to a kid when she did it. If somebody had asked my opinion at home, I'd have thought I'd stumbled into the wrong house on my way home from school.

"I don't care."

Her eyebrows shot up.

"I mean, I don't know! Anything's fine with me!"

She studied my face and saw that I meant it. "Alrighty, then. Let me think on it and see what I can come up with."

We didn't talk about the trip again until Friday. It was that sacred to me. But it was all I thought about. I guess she knew.

Friday, as I was heading out, one hand on the door, I asked, "What should I bring?" Like it had just occurred to me.

"Mmmm. Well, church clothes, for sure. I promised your mama."

I nodded.

"I don't know. Some of your nice new school clothes for traveling, I guess."

That made sense. It was all I had besides shorts and scrub clothes.

"Jammies and toothbrush." She chuckled. "I got a head start on you there." She pushed her upper plate out toward me with her tongue and slid it back into place. It took me a second to laugh. For somebody who'd had a whole lot of time to become predictable, she had a lot of surprises left.

Then she remembered something. "Billie Marie, come with me a minute, would you?" She was already headed for the stairs. I followed her up, but I hung back enough to let her take her time.

She paused on the landing to catch her breath, then opened the door to what she called "the guest room." She hadn't had any guests during my lifetime, but I suppose that's what you call a spare bedroom. I didn't know any-body else who had one.

It was the room we had used to store most of the boxes of knickknacks, so I knew it well. The roses on the wallpaper were faded to a soft pink. The bedroom set was much older and more fragile-looking than the heavy modern oak in Miss Lydia's room. A rouge-pink down comforter looked like it had floated onto the bed and it rested beneath a crocheted lace throw that had probably started out white. There was a rag rug on the floor I'd lay money had been braided downstairs in this very house. A seated vanity reflected a framed cross-stitch sampler in all three panes of the mirror. The room was old-fashioned and a little shabby, but I wished it was mine every time I was in it.

Miss Lydia opened a door to the smell of woolens and leather stored too long without a good airing. She pointed back toward a corner.

"There are three suitcases back there, child, but I can't crawl back in that short space anymore. Would you drag them out for me, please?"

I had to do the breaststroke through clothes hanging on a rod, but then I saw what she meant. The closet was open and sloped all the way out to the roofline. It made something like a closet behind the main closet. It would have made a wonderful playhouse for a kid.

The suitcases were the only things in there besides boxes sealed up with duct tape. I dragged them out, one by one.

"Hmmm." Miss Lydia studied them, hand on her chin. They were a matched set in buttery brown leather. Three sizes. "That small one is more of a cosmetics case, isn't big enough for anything to wear." She nudged the medium one with her toe. "That be big enough for the wardrobe you're planning to bring?"

"Oh, you don't need to—." Then I stopped. I hadn't once considered what I would put my belongings in. If we owned any suitcases Mama hadn't offered them up yet.

"Be easier to keep track of two if they match. Tell your folks that if they put up a fuss."

I just nodded and wondered if I would ever be as smart as she was.

I put the small case back where it had been and carried the other two into the hallway. Miss Lydia was stopped in front of the closed door to Curtis's room. She looked about ten years older.

I had never noticed how hunched she was getting in the back and it made me wonder if grief might play a part in bending an old woman over like that.

"I've just not been able to bring myself . . . I s'pose one of these days I'll have to . . ." She shook her head.

"I'll help you," I said.

"No, child!" She had never been that sharp with me. "You shouldn't have to. . . ."

I knew what she wasn't saying. I told her, "You shouldn't have to, either."

She nodded. "Lemme think on it." She took the railing and started her slow descent. "No hurry, I suppose."

I carried the two suitcases down to the kitchen. When she started soaping up the dishrag, I got an idea.

I said, "No, Miss Lydia, don't. We got some saddle soap at home. I use it on my ball glove. Let me clean these up right, and I'll bring yours back before I go to bed tonight." She smiled and waved a hand absentmindedly. I could see that part of her was still upstairs on the landing.

When Mama got home she complained that the kitchen smelled like a locker room, but I think she was mainly peeved that I hadn't cooked supper. I should have known once her feeling of power over granting me the trip had faded she was going to start feeling left out. I should have had my defenses up. While we were making cold cuts into sandwiches she said, "I wondered what you were going to put your things in."

I winced. When she caught me off guard she could still make me wonder just when it was that she decided to stop taking care of me altogether.

Chapter Fourteen

Miss Lydia was waiting at the foot of her sidewalk when Mama and I left the next morning. I had tried on everything the previous evening and settled on my favorite new outfit, but I felt like I was wearing overalls when I saw her. She had on a shirtwaist dress in an autumn-leaves print and brown old-lady shoes I'd never seen. The finishing touches were a brown velvet hat with one of those little veils in front and white wrist-length gloves.

I'd never seen white gloves outside of church occasions and it made me want to stand up straighter and call her "ma'am." I knew people dressed up to show respect for an occasion, but I had never seen that it worked the other way—clothes can draw respect, too.

Miss Lydia polished Mama's halo all the way to Milton, thanking her for letting her "good help" get away for a couple of days during the busiest season of the year.

It was what Mama needed just then and I silently blessed Miss Lydia for it.

And then we were at the station and Miss Lydia was turning our bags over to a colored man dressed like a member of a marching band and Mama was using her stern voice to warn me to behave, like otherwise I was going to give Miss Lydia trouble, and Miss Lydia was back from buying our tickets and we were climbing those shiny metal steps and deciding where to sit and waving out the window to Mama waving back and then watching her get smaller and smaller until the train rounded a curve and we couldn't see anything but muddy grain fields out any window.

The train, once it got up to full speed, had a rhythm and a sway that felt a lot different from a car. There was that to get used to and surroundings to be inspected. The conductor came around to punch our tickets and a man with skin dark as an eggplant came down the aisle selling reading material and oranges and peanuts off a cart. Miss Lydia bought a Kansas City *Star* from him and he touched the brim of his cap before he moved on.

We'd been moving a little over a half hour when Miss Lydia cleared her throat. "Billie Marie," she said, "I need to tell you something. This trip isn't entirely about sightseeing and such."

I was looking out the window and said, "Yeah, I

know. You said you had some business at a bank." When she didn't answer I turned and saw that hadn't been what she meant. The expression on her face made my heart pick up its pace.

"I made you an appointment with that Dr. Matassa I wrote to in the city. We're to be at his office this afternoon at three o'clock."

"Why?" It was no more than a squeak.

"Now, then, there's probably nothing to worry about at all." There were only six other people in the train car, but Miss Lydia was talking low. She glanced around, then said, "Here." She opened her purse and handed me an envelope. "This'll explain it better than I can and without being overheard."

It was a letter from Dr. Matassa. The first paragraph answered "your question as to whether a girl could become pregnant before her menses commence." I gulped and read, "A woman will ovulate approximately two weeks before her first, and every, period. So, yes, if she happened to have intercourse around that time, she could get pregnant and have a baby before she ever menstruated."

He went on to say the chances against it were astronomical. I had tears in my eyes, thinking, *But the odds wouldn't mean a hill of beans to you if you turned out to be the one girl in a million it happened to.*

There was more. "It would be prudent to bring the

girl in for an examination, in any case . . ." the second page began. Then my vision started swimming and I only saw single words here and there. Words about injury and diseases I'd never heard of. I didn't want to make a scene, but I couldn't stop the tears that were dripping down my face.

"Here, now," Miss Lydia said and reached into the wrist of her left glove for a small hankie. "There's no use of that now." But I could see tears welling up in her eyes as she dabbed at my cheeks. "It's likely nothing at all. Nothing at all. This is just to make sure. That's all. That's all." She was crooning like you do trying to put a baby to sleep.

"So . . . he . . . knows?" I whispered.

"Well, sort of." Miss Lydia looked past me out the window. "I was afraid that if I just asked him like I was curious about whether or not . . . you know . . ." I nodded. ". . . he might not see a need to get back to me with an answer. But I didn't exactly tell him the truth, either."

"So . . . what did you tell him?"

"That you are my granddaughter. That I am your legal guardian."

"But who did you say . . . ?" I asked.

"I didn't. I just didn't say."

"Oh." I couldn't think of any more to say so I just rode along, steeping in this new worry. Miss Lydia folded the letter back into its envelope and put it inside her pocketbook, then went back to staring out the window. Every time I snuck a quick glance, her face told me she saw nothing of the passing countryside. Finally she sighed and turned toward me with a look of resignation. "Part of the paper?" She was unfolding it.

I said, "Sure, I'll take the section with the funnies."

And I would bet you she read as many words as I did before we reached the station in Kansas City. Exactly none.

Chapter Fifteen

The Kansas City train station was about a hundred times bigger than the one in Milton and I had never been in such a bustle. I felt pretty grown-up walking alongside Miss Lydia with a suitcase in each hand like I was her personal attendant or something. But if anyone noticed us at all we probably looked like what we were pretending to be: a grandma and granddaughter. I'm sure nobody would have believed we were really a murderer and a little girl who might be pregnant.

Outside, Miss Lydia stepped to the curb and raised her hand to hail a cab, and it took work not to fall over in shock.

I guess I had pictured everyplace we were going—hotel, restaurants, theater, department store, whatever—all on the same block. I was conditioned to what you might call condensed geography. But if I *had* thought about transportation, I would have bet we'd be riding the bus.

"The Muehlbach Hotel," Miss Lydia pronounced once we were seated behind the driver in the bright yellow cab, and something caught in my throat. There were commercials for the Muehlbach on the evening news back home and it looked like the fanciest place in the world.

I had brought ten dollars with me from the Lydia wages I'd saved, and I began to wish I'd brought all I had. "Miss Lydia, just so you know," I whispered, "I'd be fine someplace cheaper."

She answered in full voice, "Well, I wouldn't." She turned to me and her eyes sparkled. "Just so you know."

Some sort of wordless ceremony took place when we pulled up in front of the Muehlbach. I felt like I was in one of those dreams where you find yourself on stage but you haven't learned the dance steps. Our bags were out and on the sidewalk, money changed hands, a uniformed man materialized and took our luggage inside. A man dressed like a military officer opened a brass-trimmed door next to the revolving door spinning with folks hurrying around and around and Miss Lydia inclined her chin when the doorman tipped his hat. I kept my mouth shut and tried not to fall down.

The lobby was everything it looked like on TV and more. Chandeliers twinkled like stars, the colors were richer, the huge tropical plants greener. I had seen it so many times it felt like I'd been there before.

Miss Lydia, head high, looked neither left nor right. She marched to the front desk where the man who had taken our bags was standing at attention. She slipped something from her glove into his palm. He nodded and smiled before striding away.

She pulled off her gloves, finger by finger, and arranged them on the marble counter. She turned to me and winked.

"Yes, ma'am, how can I help you?" The man behind the desk had hair the color of gunmetal and sounded like he enjoyed listening to his own voice.

"Mrs. Avery Jenkins," Miss Lydia replied, "and her granddaughter. You will find we have reservations." Miss Lydia hadn't been talking like herself ever since we left Milton. Now she sounded like an old-time movie star.

The man did a double take too. "Mrs. Jenkins," he said. His tone was twenty degrees warmer than before. "Of course. It's been too long since you've graced us with your presence."

"I've not been back since I lost Mr. Jenkins. That's just over seven years now."

The man bowed his head for a couple of seconds. He would have made a good preacher. They usually like the sound of their own voices too, and he had the sympathetic look down pat. But maybe he reminded me of church just because I could smell the carnation in his lapel and it reminded me of funerals.

"Our sincere condolences," the man intoned. Their nods to one another were so deep it was almost a bow. "Let us see what we can do to make your stay with us as pleasant as possible."

Another dance took place with me trying not to make any stupid steps, and we were in an elevator with mirrors on all the walls. Then we were getting out on the twelfth floor and stopping before a door marked 1214. The man carrying our suitcases put a key in the knob and ushered us in with a grand sweeping motion.

It was a beautiful room, and two king-sized beds looked small in all that space. But the Muehlbach showed their rooms on TV, too, so I had the weird feeling of it seeming familiar.

After the door closed Miss Lydia walked to the window and threw open the drapes. "Our favorite room," she said.

I went and stood beside her. We had a clear view of the buildings in downtown Kansas City and could see beyond them all the way to the river. It was the farthest I had ever been from the ground and it took my breath away.

After some minutes I remembered, though. "Uh, Miss Lydia?"

"Mmm-mm?" She tore herself away like she was lost in a dream.

"What's with your voice?"

"My voice? Why, child? What's wrong with my voice?"

"Nothing's *wrong,* ma'am." I had never called her "ma'am" before. That's how off-balance I was. "And it's not your voice, really. You just don't sound anything like you do at home. You're not acting it, either."

"I'm not at home." She gave me a strange little smile.

"But . . ." I frowned.

She laughed and took my hands in hers. "Do you mean because I'm saying 'aren't' instead of 'ain't'? 'Saying' instead of 'sayin'?"

"Yeah, I guess that's pretty much it," I answered.

"It doesn't make me a different person, you know. There's no need to look so frightened." She laughed again.

I hugged myself. "Are you pretending you're from the city or something?"

"Not really," she said, looking out the window again. "At least no more than I pretend I'm from Cumberland when I'm there."

I wrestled with this and lost.

She sighed. "Billie Marie," she said, "I don't feel like I'm pretending anything anytime. I just find it easier to breathe, wherever I am, as a fish in the water rather than out."

I stared at her like I'd never seen her before.

"You've watched *The Beverly Hillbillies*?" Miss Lydia's mouth was puckered.

I nodded.

"Why do people think that show is funny?" She cocked her head like a bird.

Those people were so backward and ignorant, it was comical. They had absolutely no idea how life in a big city worked. And then I knew what she meant.

To some people we would be the hillbillies. I had never thought of that and my face got warm. "But, then," I asked her, "why talk the way you do back home? Shouldn't you just be yourself all the time so people know who you really are?"

"That is who I am. So is this. I know who I am, and that's all that really matters." She turned to make sure her words got through to me. "Listen to me. If I spoke like this in Cumberland, what would—your mother, for example—think?"

"Well . . ." It took a moment to get Mama's voice in my head. "She'd think you were uppity. That you thought you were better than everybody else around."

Miss Lydia nodded. "But when I 'land o' Goshen' her . . ."

"She just thinks you're . . . an old lady."

She threw back her head and laughed. "And that I am. That I am. An old lady who learned a long time ago that fish have an easier time of it in the water than out." She patted my shoulder. "Well, lovely girl, I'm hungry. What say we go find some lunch?"

I nodded, ready to follow her. But my head was trying to put together a puzzle somewhere about eighty miles to the northeast. I still couldn't quite reconcile the Miss Lydia I knew in Cumberland with the one standing in front of me.

We walked a couple of blocks to Putsch's Cafeteria. It felt funny to stand in a herd at the corner waiting for an electric signal to change color and give us our "mother, may I" to cross the street. Miss Lydia kept one hand on my elbow. Whether it was for my sake or hers, I was glad of it.

The only cafeteria I had ever seen was at school, so this one stopped me short. There was a glass case a mile long and the whole distance was paved with single servings on saucers. It was like every Sunday dinner in history all at once. I stepped back to let Miss Lydia go first.

As she got her tray and silverware she told me, "Get whatever you want, Billie Marie. I don't whoop it up very often anymore, so there's no need to be shy this weekend."

I was so overwhelmed with choices I ended up

watching and taking what she did—roast beef with gravy, some kind of cheesy potato dish, peas and carrots cooked together, and a slice of banana-cream pie. At the cash register she saw it and laughed. "Are you sure you don't want another pass at it?" she said.

"No thank you, ma'am." I knew I was blushing.

We settled into a booth and Miss Lydia put a cloth napkin in her lap. I followed suit, monkey see. She took a sip of iced tea and cleared her throat. She looked at her plate and said, "I hate to bring this up right now, but we have to decide. What is your name going to be?"

"Huh?" She had turned into someone else on this trip. Was I expected to change, too?

"At the doctor's office. They're going to want to make a chart on you, and I think it might be best if it were not in your true name. Don't you think?"

I hadn't, but I did then. "Sure."

"Since you're to be my granddaughter, we can keep it simple and make your last name same as mine. What first name would you take, given a choice?"

Well, it wouldn't be William. I thought for a minute and said, "Lucy."

Hearing the name of her childhood friend moistened her eyes. "I do love you, child," she said.

"I love you too." I felt as much sadness in my smile as I could see in hers.

❧ ❧ ❧

The doctor's office was in the Country Club Plaza and we had to take another cab to get there. Out the window the view changed from the gritty downtown district to streets paved with brick and elaborate fountains everywhere you looked. Buildings sat lower, no more than three or four stories high. The atmosphere felt like the ritzy aunt of the neighborhood we had just left.

At five minutes to three we walked up to the desk in Dr. Matassa's office and Miss Lydia announced us. She was handed a clipboard and we were finishing up the forms when a nurse called, "Lucy Jenkins." Miss Lydia stood up, but it took me a second to remember they meant me.

We were shown to an examining room and the nurse handed me a paper gown. "Everything off," she said, "and this ties in front." She frowned at Miss Lydia and looked back to me. "Are you sure you want your grandmother here for the examination?"

"Yes!" we answered. She nodded and left. Miss Lydia turned her back and pretended to be interested in an anatomical chart on the wall while I changed.

Dr. Matassa was the youngest doctor I had ever seen. He was not much taller than me and slight of build, with black hair in tight curls and eyes so dark you couldn't see the pupils. He introduced himself and started reading through my chart. He frowned.

He looked at Miss Lydia. "You sent me the letter?"

She nodded.

He turned to me. "You were raped." Miss Lydia and I had never used that word. It felt like a kick in the stomach.

"Yes," I whispered. Miss Lydia nodded some more.

Then he asked. Of course he would. "Who did this?"

Miss Lydia and I whipped our heads around to search one another for an answer. "Why does that matter?" she croaked.

Dr. Matassa looked perturbed. "There are laws in this country against having intercourse with a girl—" he flipped a page on my chart and read "—eleven years old. For good reason. Part of caring for this patient means seeing that the proper authorities are notified."

Miss Lydia looked as horrified as I was. We had gotten this far holding ourselves together around the secret between us. And now—because she had wanted to do what was best for me—everything was threatening to come crashing down.

The mind is a funny thing. Sometimes it takes forever to process one thought. Other times it runs through a whole day's worth in a matter of seconds.

First thought: If either of us answered the doctor truthfully, Miss Lydia was going to jail. Because if anybody learned anything, everybody would figure out everything.

Second thought: I could say, "That's okay. We don't really need an examination. We'll just go now." But we had put Miss Lydia's real address on the forms. He could call the county sheriff's office and describe us.

I thought about grabbing the chart and my clothes and just running. But he might have Miss Lydia's letter somewhere in a file. Her address again.

And besides, *she* wasn't going to outrun him.

I saw her expression settle into sad acceptance and wanted to scream.

"It was—" she said.

"It was my brother!" I yelled.

They both jumped.

"Well, my stepbrother, anyway. That's why I was sent to live with Grandma Jenkins here. My . . . stepmother, she took his side against me when he told her nothing happened. She talked my father into sending me away. Said I was a troublemaker."

I sounded like I had just run a mile. "So it wouldn't do any good to call anybody and besides, they live all the way over in Springfield, Illinois." I sat blinking, trying to get my breath under control.

Miss Lydia held my hand during the examination and made small talk while I told myself it was no more embarrassing than a trip to the dentist. It's a pretty personal thing when someone looks around in your mouth, too. Everybody goes through that. I tried to pretend this was nothing more.

Dr. Matassa "hmmmed" a lot and told me he was taking a swab from inside me to send to the lab. I saw him wipe something onto a little square piece of glass and put it on the counter just before he snapped off his gloves. Then he told me to get dressed and he'd be right back.

As soon as the door closed, Miss Lydia and I collapsed into a hug. She rocked me back and forth, saying what a good girl I was, telling me "thank you" over and over. Like the lies hadn't been for my own sake as well as hers.

The doctor came back and said there didn't seem to be any injury. We nodded like we were encouraging him. He said they would need a urine sample for a pregnancy test. Then they'd draw blood for some other tests and we'd be done.

Miss Lydia spoke up before I could find my voice. "When will you have the results?" she asked.

"You can call my nurse Tuesday morning." And he was gone.

Chapter Sixteen

You know those big tests that you spend more time dreading than studying for? How you walk out ready to burst into song before you even know if you flunked, you're so glad to have them over with? That's how Miss Lydia and I were when we hit the sidewalk of the Country Club Plaza. We laughed and talked at the same time and hugged some more. Then she suggested ice cream sundaes and we were off to find some.

That night, after a matinee showing of *Charly* at the Midland Theater—which looked like I imagine the inside of a castle—and after steak and lobster at the Savoy Grille, and after we had taken turns in the bathroom and come out in nightgowns, and after Miss Lydia had started snoring, I climbed out of bed and cracked the drapes open far enough to peek out.

It was a fairyland of lights. There was so much movement in the streets and the skies it made me dizzy. I wondered what all those people were doing that time of night other than wanting to be somewhere they weren't.

I looked at Miss Lydia in the dim light. She was flat on her back, her skin smoothed out so that it looked like wax. It hit like a bullet to the heart—I would most likely stand at her coffin one day and see her just like that.

And I realized in that moment that no matter what else happened, when Miss Lydia died the hurt that we shared was all going to belong to me.

I prayed. "Not yet, God, please. Please let me have her as long as you can."

We went to Mass the next morning at a cathedral worthy of the pope. It started at ten, same as back home. Strange to know those words were being spoken in the exact same ceremony in churches all around the world.

In the taxi on the way to the train station, Miss Lydia told me she had enjoyed the music. I asked what church she belonged to.

"Hmmm. Well, I was raised Lutheran," she said, "but I wouldn't say I'm affiliated with any one religion now." She looked the way you're supposed to after church. Pleasant and serene.

"Why not?" I thought she didn't go just because she didn't drive.

"Well, it got so it seemed that my church, *all* churches for that matter, had a lot more to do with raising money and enforcing silly man-made rules than they had to do with God. I guess you could say I cut out the middleman."

I'd been taught that even people who belonged to a religion other than mine were headed for hell when they died. Being religious without any church at all was so foreign a thought that I put it aside to ponder later.

Miss Lydia was so quiet on the train I was almost glad to be going home. I hoped she was just tired. We had taken cabs everywhere, but I knew she had still done more walking in two days than she had in the month before.

I didn't mind not talking. I was busy enough anyway, back on track trying to protect my fate with all-out attention. I started making bargains with the Virgin Mary. I'd say the rosary every day. I'd use every last dollar Miss Lydia had paid me to light candles to her in church. Please just let me not be pregnant.

I talked some to God, too, but it seemed easier to pray to a woman just then.

I did trouble Miss Lydia once. A few miles out of Milton I laid my hand on her arm and waited. She turned with a question in her eyes.

"Miss Lydia?" I said. "When we're home, do you have to talk to me like I'm one of the hillbillies?"

She smiled every so slightly and patted my hand. "No,

child, I suppose I don't," she said. "Just don't be surprised if you have to remind me once and again."

Mama was waiting for us on the platform. "Land o' Goshen, Miriam!" was how Miss Lydia greeted her, and I saw the least little wink aimed my way. "Take pity on a couple of stragglers and haul our poor, worn-out carcasses home!" And so she did.

Chapter Seventeen

I had never understood people who were afraid to go to the doctor because they thought something terrible might be wrong with them. As though not knowing made it less real. It just didn't make sense.

Until that Tuesday morning.

Dr. Matassa had told Miss Lydia to call for test results then and all the relief I'd felt with the appointment behind me disappeared in the dread of that phone call. If I was pregnant, knowing it wasn't going to make me any more so, but the knot in my belly gave me a whole new appreciation for those "hear no evil, see no evil" monkeys.

Monday was bad enough—Miss Lydia and I sat at noon and pushed food around on our plates, so distracted we were answering questions the other hadn't asked and asking questions the other had just answered.

Finally she'd said, "Let's go see what's on TV." And we

sat in her living room until six o'clock staring at the screen. I could have been threatened at knifepoint later and still wouldn't have been able to recite one line of dialogue from a show or commercial that day. And I'd bet Miss Lydia would have done no better.

Tuesday morning I woke up at gray dawn and tried to hypnotize myself back to sleep watching the second hand jerk its way around the face of my bedside clock. 6:36, 6:37, 6:38—I agonized sixty times a minute all the way until 8:11. Then I must have fallen back to sleep because, when I looked again, it was 11:51. I jumped up, threw on some clothes, and ran out the door without even brushing my hair or my teeth.

Jewel Wilkerson was standing at the service window of the post office chewing some subject to death with Lewis McEntire, and I thanked God Miss Lydia had given me the combination to her box way back when she and I owned the town. I twirled the dial on hers, then ours, and ran out of there with an armload of mail so fast those other two probably wondered at the breeze that ruffled their hair.

I didn't stop by home—I just ran to Miss Lydia's with my arms full and made it through her back door using an elbow and a knee. She was standing at the stove and I announced myself by saying, "WELL?" a whole lot louder than I meant to.

She jumped like I'd fired a starting pistol and turned around with eyes wide and a hand on her heart. "Lands, child!" she said, and I mumbled some apology.

"Well?" I tried again, much softer.

She stood blinking. "I haven't called yet," she said. "I thought I'd wait until after we ate."

I stood and stared for so long she wilted and gave me a resigned little nod. She turned the burners off under the pans on the stove and fumbled with her purse and her glasses. I wanted to scream at her to hurry, old woman! but then I saw how her hands were shaking and felt like a heel.

Twice she misdialed and had to start over, and I thought I might faint until I remembered to breathe. When Miss Lydia snapped to attention I knew someone had answered on the other end, and I concentrated on in, out, deep and slow, while she identified herself and nodded into the receiver.

Then she put her hand over the mouthpiece and stage-whispered, "They're transferring me." In, out, slow and deep.

She told her name again and mentioned a Lucy Jenkins I finally remembered was me. Then she was nodding again and saying "Uh-huh, I see" and "That's good" and "I'm so glad to hear that."

I was about to let out a whoop when Miss Lydia's

brows folded in on one another and a cloud came across her face. "But—but—" she said, and my knees started to wobble. "But how could that happen?" she was asking the phone. I felt behind me for a chair. "But we—I don't know how—yes, I see, but—" Her elbows were on the counter and she leaned her weight on them.

My heart felt like a fist in my chest. Miss Lydia waited, then sighed and said, "Well, I'll have to talk to . . . my granddaughter and get back to you. Uh-huh. Yes, I know." She hung up, held her face in her hands for a couple of seconds and turned to me with the worst fake smile I'd ever seen. I wanted to die.

She crumpled into a chair facing me and took my hands in hers. "There's good news," she said, and I was not about to buy a syllable of that. "All of the blood tests came back fine," she went on. "None of the . . . diseases they tested for were positive."

Yeah, well, pregnancy might end my life as I knew it but it didn't qualify as a disease, and I knew she was holding out. "What else?" I accused her.

She caught her bottom lip in her teeth and shook her head. "They're saying they . . . mislocated the urine sample and need another one in order to run the pregnancy test."

"They LOST IT?" I almost knocked my chair over backward—Miss Lydia pulled me back upright.

"That's what they're saying." Her face looked like a wreck and I knew it was a mirror of mine. "I . . . just don't know whether to believe them or not."

The gears in my head were grinding. "You think they know whether or not I'm pregnant and won't tell us?" I asked her. "That doesn't make any sense. Why would they do that?"

"No. . . ." I saw a fleck of fear behind her glasses. "It doesn't make sense. But that doctor was awfully keen on notifying the authorities, if you recall, and most doctors I've ever known think they're close enough to God that they don't like to be told 'no.'"

I turned this over a few times. "They want me to come back."

Miss Lydia nodded.

"And this time they'll have somebody there waiting for me."

She shook her head. "It wouldn't surprise me. I just don't know."

I clenched and unclenched my fists. "So, what do we do now?" I asked.

"I guess we wait," Miss Lydia said and she found a spot to study on the floor. I gave it my attention too.

Neither of us drove a car and we could hardly go back to the city without Mama suspecting something. So it wasn't like we could go to a different doctor. I looked up at Miss Lydia and she nodded like she was reading my thoughts. "Nothing else to do," she said. I just swallowed, hard.

But the sun went down that night and came up the next morning just the same as it would if we already knew what was going to happen to me. Miss Lydia and I went on doing our best to live as close to normal as we could. It was all we could do. Besides wait.

Chapter Eighteen

The following Monday was Labor Day. Miss Lydia made a special lunch, chicken fricassee, trying to jolly me up about going back to school the next day, but I was having none of that. I had always hated going back to school before—and this year I was going back in a woman's body with God knows what going on inside it. To me it felt more like I was headed to the gallows.

My moping finally got to Miss Lydia enough that she got cross. "Land, child, I don't know what to do with you. You got a life to live, you know, no matter what else happens, and school will at least give you something else to think about. Other people to look at and talk to besides me. Why, I used to get almost as excited about first day of school as I did about Christmas."

"You had friends." That sounded pathetic even to my own ears.

She let out a spew of exasperation. "Well, I'm afraid you're just going to have to try."

I gave her my best basset-hound look. "You're trying to get rid of me, aren't you?" All I needed was violin music.

"Billie Marie." She stared over my shoulder with her mouth set, like she was making herself count to ten. "You still have your ruby heart?"

Of course I did. I smiled and her face settled into familiar creases. As long as I had her, I'd manage. Somehow.

Tuesday morning I changed outfits three times and still couldn't decide which one showed my figure least. When I got to school, Karen and Debbie, the other two girls going into sixth grade, were sitting together inside on the steps, same as every day I could remember. I smiled and said hi, then ducked into the classroom before they could not answer me.

This year was my return trip to the fifth- and sixth-grade room and the only joy in that was already being used to Miss Wilson. The even-numbered grades are a drag. Half the classroom is kids a year younger and dorkier than you and, unless you're one of the slow ones, you've seen all the coming attractions the year before.

If you're not stupid, the only challenge in an even-numbered grade is if you have a new teacher. And only then if it's an especially serious nutcase.

Most of the teachers Cumberland attracts are like most of the priests who come to Milton. They're either starry-eyed new recruits who believe they can change the world if only they can get everybody to *pull together!* and *be enthusiastic!* and they last about a year. Or they're at the end of a career that doesn't beg too much close examination.

I was in for a boring year, but at least Miss Wilson was a predictable bore.

She's a vague woman, soft-spoken and more than a little nervous. She smells like cigarettes and always gives the impression her mind is somewhere else. I imagine she'll be at Cumberland Consolidated until she retires, being pretty short in the gumption department. I know she was married for a while but it's hard to picture. There just doesn't seem to be enough person there to account for half of a couple.

Most of the fifth-grade boys were milling around the classroom that morning showing off whatever their new big deal was. One had a new watch, the kind scuba divers wear. That was going to come in handy in the middle of Missouri. One had a new scar and another had a bigger scar. When Joe Kloppinger started unbuckling his belt, I quit watching.

Nobody from my class was there just then, although

several of the desks on the sixth-grade side had already been claim-staked with jackets or notebooks. I was glad to see my first choice still up for grabs.

I like a window seat as a hedge against boredom and I like the last row so I don't always feel like somebody is staring at the back of my head. I sat down and took a quick look at everything carved into my new desk by previous squatters. Then I took a look around the room, like Miss Lydia had told me to. Like I had promised.

There were four girls in the class a year behind me and at the moment they were huddled in the back of the room. Carol Dobbs was holding forth with the other three listening. Cheryl Schroeder had a rhythm going between digging in her nose and wiping her skirt. Linda Hines looked like a mechanical robot set to bite each fingernail and spit it to the side. Bite. Spit. Bite. Spit. Sherry Day had a hank of hair twisted so tight around her index finger I could see the little bald spot she had come by over the years.

Then the fifth-grade boys started a shoulder-punching contest, yelling, "You flinched!" "Did not!" "Did too!" I wished Miss Lydia could see it with her own eyes so she wouldn't think I was exaggerating later.

The bell rang and kids started filing in. There were five boys in my class, and none of them appeared to have changed over the summer—not a solitary whit. It didn't seem possible, but not a one of them looked so much as one millimeter taller. In fact, I calculated I was probably as tall now as Paul Harding. He had always towered over everybody our age.

Then Karen and Debbie came in and I realized how dim the hallway light had been. They were wearing the same skirt and blouse set in only slightly different color schemes. Both wore iridescent blue eye shadow, navy-blue mascara, and so much foundation it looked like they'd spray-painted their faces bubble-gum pink. They were in full bloom. I had to open my desk and pretend to look for something to hide my grin.

Miss Wilson materialized at the front of the room and rapped on her desk with a ruler before launching into her "welcome back, here's what to expect, now let's get down to work" speech. She might have blinked a few times when she got a load of Karen and Debbie, but it's hard to say. She seemed to be concentrating on something she wasn't saying. I tuned out when a robin landed in the open windowsill not three feet from me. He and I started turning our heads side to side in a mirrored dance.

The word "teams" got my attention. ". . . and so the principal has decided to get a running start at it, if you will, by starting the Constitution in sixth grade and using seventh to really polish that knowledge before taking the state test."

I hadn't caught the part that explained the "teams" idea, but it was clear the class was pairing off. Karen and Debbie exchanged a knowing glance. The Johnson twins punched each other in the arm. Paul Harding and Rick Waters shook hands across the aisle.

That left only Harlan Willits and me—and when that fact dawned on him he turned around and gaped at me with as much horror as I felt. Karen and Debbie twittered like parakeets. I felt the heat climb my neck and continue up to my scalp.

"Twice a week we'll set aside time for teams to find a spot outside the classroom to discuss the week's chapters without disrupting others. . . ." Outside the classroom. Twice a week. I didn't hear anything else until the bell rang for recess.

At least this would be my last year to suffer recess. I shuffled out the back door and sat down on the step with a book, same as I'd done twice a day for years. Most of the boys were already on the baseball diamond and the girls were split up into their usual coveys. There was yelling and laughing and the occasional indignant shriek. Every recess sounded exactly the same, every day, every year.

A pair of Keds appeared in front of me. I looked up from my book and found Harlan Willits pounding a fist into the pocket of his baseball glove.

"Hey, come help us out," he said. "We need one more to make teams."

I was too astonished to speak. I looked past him and saw the other boys standing in two groups, looking our way like they expected something.

I shook my head.

"Oh, c'mon. You gonna sit here all by yourself *and* keep us from being able to play?"

I said, "Girls don't . . . you know." Fourth grade, like punching a time clock, girls stopped using the playground equipment *and* playing baseball. Everybody knew that.

"We're not asking girls. Just you. And it's not like it's a *law*."

"But I haven't played since—"

"You'll still be better than the runts."

"I don't have a glove."

"There's plenty to go around."

"I'm left-handed."

"So's Bobby Johnson. We'll put you on opposite teams."

I had run out of arguments. I marked my page and started following Harlan out to the field. The other boys would protest. They would come up with a better idea. I wouldn't have to play.

Then something really awful occurred to me. "Hey,

Harlan," I yelled toward his back. "Just because we have to study together, you know, it doesn't mean anything."

He spun around and walked backward, wearing a look that could wilt jimson weed. He said, "Gee, I'll try to wait till after Christmas to ask you to marry me." Then he spun forward and left me to blush at his back.

"Did you have fun?" That was the first thing Miss Lydia asked that afternoon when the day started tumbling out of me.

"Well, yeah . . . yeah, I did." It was still a wonder. Once the game was underway, I was just one of them. I had done pretty well, too—got on base every time I batted and even tagged Bobby Johnson out at second with his own glove.

But that wasn't the point. I was trying to explain to Miss Lydia the utter horror of this team-studying business and she just wasn't getting it. I tried another tack. "But to be the only boy-girl study team—people will think we're some kind of freaks."

"What people?"

"The other girls."

"The other two in your class? Did they ask the teacher to make an exception and put you with them?"

"Well, no. . . ."

"Well, then, they know you had no choice in the matter. Why do you care what they think, anyway?"

Because there are two of them and one of me, I thought. They have the strength of the majority. And the power to ridicule is a mighty thing.

But I knew Miss Lydia would say that was rubbish. She was good at turning an old idea inside out to reveal its stupidity. So I kept quiet. She might be right, but it still felt wrong. She had forgotten what it was like.

"Sounds like you might have some fun studying, anyway. This Harlan sounds like a character."

"Huh?" Harlan Willits was white paint. A clean chalkboard. Solid color wallpaper. Nothing.

Miss Lydia chuckled. "Well, you have to admit, that crack about asking you to marry him was a pretty good comeback."

It was, when I reconsidered. Where did I get off anyway, afraid Harlan *meant* something by asking me to fill out the baseball field? In class he had looked mortified to be teamed up with me. I wasn't sure whether that should come as a relief or an embarrassment.

"Give it a chance, anyway, Billie Marie," Miss Lydia was saying. "You're only young once—don't forget to have some fun."

Right. I faked a smile, gathered her trash, and said good-bye. I didn't feel like telling her just then about walking into the lunchroom that day. My first time in it since I had run out of it bleeding.

How the smell of the room brought it all back. How my mouth suddenly tasted like stale cigarettes and coffee. How I had to sit with my head between my knees all through lunch period because I felt like I was either going to pass out or throw up.

Nor did I feel like telling her about my last exchange of the day with Harlan. Walking back toward the schoolhouse after second recess, he had fallen into step beside me and said, "Hey, you got a stomachache or something?"

And I'd said, "Oh, no. I just wasn't hungry at lunch, that's all."

And he'd said, "That's not what I meant. I just wondered why you keep poking at your stomach like you do."

Chapter Nineteen

A week later I was sick to death of school and told Miss Lydia so. I had studied the Constitution with Harlan a couple of times, if you could call it that when the two of us sat in opposite corners of the room with our noses in our books. But otherwise, every day felt like a rerun all day long. The end of May was at least ten years away.

"It seems like at least current events would be new," Miss Lydia said. "It isn't like history repeats itself *that* quickly." She chuckled at her own joke, but I felt too low even to humor her.

"We don't study current events," I explained. "Too bogged down in history, I guess."

"What?" Miss Lydia squawked so loudly it woke me up some. "They aren't teaching you to pay attention to the world around you?"

I didn't think so.

"Well, how are you supposed to take over when it's

your turn?" she asked. The idea of anybody I knew at Cumberland Consolidated taking over anything was so funny I nearly fell out of my chair.

She didn't laugh with me. In fact, she looked pretty sore. "There's not any one of you aiming to grow up someday?"

I said, "Someday, sure." But I didn't understand what she meant and she looked like she was trying to think of words that could penetrate my thick head.

"*Time* magazine," she said finally. She looked pleased with the announcement.

I said, "Yeah, I noticed you get *Time* every week." I was bringing her mail to her every day after school. It wasn't getting any easier for her to get around on her feet. "What about it?"

"From now on you're going to take each one with you as soon as I'm through with it and after you read it we'll talk about what's going on in the world."

It sounded like a lot of work. "Oh, I don't think—"

"Oh yes, you are. You don't have to be sitting in a brick building at a desk to learn, you know. Most of my education came from being married to Mr. Jenkins." Her face lit up when she mentioned him. "We read books and he talked with me about them like I had a mind as fine as his. . . . I learned a lot when we traveled together, too. Yes, sir. If that school won't bother to give you an education, I'll just take on the project myself."

I didn't want to be anybody's project and I told her so. Then I said, "And besides, don't I have any say in the matter? I thought we were friends."

She thought for a few seconds. Estimating my fee, I imagine. "Pretty, pretty, pretty please with sugar and cream on top?" This with her hands clasped under her chin and without the hint of a smile.

I cracked up and she started laughing, too. I said, "Okay. I'll give it a try, anyway."

That night I read my first article about the war in Vietnam. I understood the individual words, but for all the sense it made to me it might have been written in French.

As it turned out, we'd have many other things to discuss before we got around to Vietnam anyway.

The next day I felt so punk I thought I might be coming down with something. I caught Harlan watching me feel my stomach and it hit me like lightning—I was starting to show symptoms. No doubt about it. The rest of the day I felt achy and lethargic and on the verge of tears. Even when I wasn't contemplating my future. Or lack of it.

I was starving by lunchtime and wolfed my food so fast I felt miserable. Even Miss Wilson noticed something was wrong. She said, "Billie? Are you feeling poorly?" and two big fat tears rolled down my cheeks before I could stop them.

I just shook my head and bit my bottom lip. What

could I say? Any mention of being sick would mean a phone call home. A phone call home would require an explanation, maybe even a trip to the doctor.

I couldn't say a word, even though it was becoming clear this was a secret I would not be able to keep much longer. I had been scared of being pregnant ever since I'd found out it might be possible. But I never had got so far as "then what?"

Miss Lydia had told me to let her think on it and I had.

I slumped through the afternoon feeling fat and hopeless. Things had started getting somewhat peaceful at home, and now I was going to bring home The Worst News a Daughter Can Tell You. Age eleven years, ten months would beat the old Cumberland record by nearly four years. I'd be one of those girls people talked about the rest of their lives. The example mothers used to keep their daughters from ruining their lives.

Then there was the poison icing on the cake—if this came out in the open, I'd have to name a name. There would be no getting around that.

Everybody and their dog would know what Curtis had done to me, but I'd be the only one to focus on. The only one they'd look at and whisper about. And the women of Cumberland counted to nine so well and so often, it wouldn't take long for them to figure out a "when" to go with the "what." Once they were there, it wouldn't be more than a mayfly's life before everyone decided Curtis's death had not been an accident after all.

I'd have to go away. That was all there was to it. I'd have to tell Mama and Daddy. My life still wouldn't be worth much, but at least they couldn't turn Miss Lydia in. Not without letting the whole world know what had happened, and they wouldn't do that for their own sake. They'd have to find a home somewhere or somebody to take me in.

Either I went away or Miss Lydia would have to. I was pretty sure they wouldn't let you off for murder even if you were older than Adam and had killed somebody worthless.

After all we had done, it was going to get away from us anyway. We wouldn't be able to stick together. I didn't bother wiping the tears away at that thought. I just sat at my desk in the back row and leaked trails down my face all through fifth-grade math. Sitting in the back row there was nobody to see me but Miss Wilson. She either didn't notice or didn't care.

I stopped by home after school to regroup before facing Miss Lydia and made a discovery that boosted my bad nerves up to a panic. I made a beeline across the street, jabbering like a chimpanzee before Miss Lydia even got the door all the way open. She made me slow down, then started getting all worked up herself. She told me to show her. I couldn't, so I ran back home.

I couldn't show her my panties while I was wearing them. I just couldn't. I put them in a paper bag, pulled on a clean pair, and ran back to find Miss Lydia holding the door open. She ripped the bag from my hand, tore it open, and burst out crying.

It was worse than I thought. "What? What's wrong with me?" I started blubbering too.

She said, "Lands, child. Oh, my sweet, sweet girl. Oh, lord," and she pulled me into a bear hug.

"*What*, Miss Lydia? *Please!*"

She took off her glasses and mopped her face with a handkerchief before she collapsed into a kitchen chair. "Oh, honey, you really don't know, do you?"

I thought I had made that clear. For want of words I shook my hands like they were on fire.

"You're menstruating," she said. "You've got your first monthly."

I wasn't ready to accept that. "That—" I pointed at the sack. "That's *not* what that is!" Whatever I really had was so bad she couldn't say it out loud.

Her voice got gentle and she said, "It doesn't always look like you'd expect, Billie Marie. I should have known your mama wouldn't tell you and told you myself. But especially at first, it doesn't always look like what it is."

It started to sink in. "But that means—" The seed hadn't sprouted. It wasn't there anymore. There was no Curtis, no baby. . . . There was nothing but *me* inside me. My belly wasn't going to announce Miss Lydia's and my secret to the whole world after all.

I stumbled into a chair. All that had changed in the last few seconds grew to such enormous proportions so fast I felt a jolt that raised goose pimples on my arms. I didn't start crying so much as explode into tears and Miss Lydia joined me.

We just bawled—there's no other word loud enough to describe it. Then we joined hands across the table and smiled wet, mottled-face smiles at each other. Then we bawled some more.

I had gotten my future back. It was going to be mine after all.

Miss Lydia and I had not tiptoed anywhere close to the subject since that day the doctor's office told her they'd lost my test.

But sitting there bawling in her kitchen made it pretty clear just how present the question had been in each of our minds.

Miss Lydia was put out with me at first when I blubbered on about how terrified I'd been that I'd have to go away. She said, "I thought we had agreed we could talk about anything?"

"Same to you," I told her.

We sat and looked at each other accusingly. Finally she sighed and said, "Well then, can we also agree that keeping a secret all to yourself comes with a heavy price tag?"

"Agreed." It sure had for me.

"And in this case it was a cost neither one of us could really afford?"

I nodded. We'd needed each other and both gone without.

"Okay. Then how about we make a pact right here and now that from now on we just trust each other?"

I swallowed and nodded.

It took a long time that night for sleep to come. I had stayed at Miss Lydia's till my folks came home, then pulled Mama into the bathroom to tell her. At first she blew out an exasperated sigh that raised the hair up off her forehead. Then she shook her head with her lips pressed into a thin line—like this was something I'd chosen to do and it was all to aggravate her. Then she showed me what to do and assured me that yes, it was that uncomfortable and I'd get used to it. I wasn't sure about that part.

Daddy acted so embarrassed later that I knew she had told him. It felt a little like being naked at the doctor's office—there was nothing officially wrong about it, but it felt kind of creepy anyway. I stayed as far away from him as I could.

It was bedtime before I was finally alone to think. First thing, I thanked God even though I was bent double with cramps by then. Then I said ten Hail Marys for good measure. And ten more after that.

I spent some time that night thinking about this new part of my life. I did some multiplying and figured I was going to have over four hundred fifty periods before they stopped. Whether I liked it or said "whoa, Nelly" didn't matter. They would come.

I couldn't imagine that any of the future four-fifty-plus would carry the emotional freight of this first one. But I had never considered the possibility that any of them would. No doubt there were millions of women staring at their bedroom ceilings at that very moment either because their period had come or because it hadn't.

I had entered the "childbearing years." Every cycle of the moon, my body was going to remind me that it was designed as a baby-making machine.

I felt so much wonder. More than a little disgust, as well. Noble and beastly both at the same time. It was like being a member of a sorority with millions of members who hadn't elected to join.

And I had a whole lot more questions for Miss Lydia.

Chapter Twenty

She had baked gingersnaps the next afternoon that were still warm when I brought her the mail. She was humming, too, and I realized she really had been a lot more worried than she had let on. We sat and munched and made jokes about my day at school for half an hour before I got to the point.

"I gotta ask you about something," I started.

"Sure, dumplin'. About what?" She was practically giggly.

"Intercourse."

Well. If you ever want to stop a room dead silent and get some undivided attention, I could suggest using that word. It hadn't sounded all that powerful when Dr. Matassa used it, but it must have just seemed tame in the same conversation as "rape." Right now Miss Lydia looked like a frog on the business end of a gig.

"You said we could talk about anything." I could feel

myself blushing and it was making me furious.

"We can. We most surely can." She looked like she was reminding herself to blink. "You just shifted gears on me a little abruptly, that's all."

We sat with our hands in our laps looking at each other. There was a fair amount of expectation in the air. After a couple of minutes, she cleared her throat. "What exactly was it you wanted to know about—it?"

"Everything!" I blurted out. Then we both let out the kind of nervous chuckle that doesn't signify anything funny has ever happened in the history of the known universe.

I backed up. "No," I said. "It's just that I never knew— or at least I didn't realize I knew—until that day you first asked about my, um, 'monthlies,' just how babies got started. Mama kind of skipped over that part."

"I imagine a lot of mamas have trouble talking about that part. Mine sure did." Miss Lydia stared into the distance and then nodded like she was making up her mind. "Okay, where do you want to start?"

I shrugged. Sometimes you feel like you don't even know enough to form a halfway decent question.

Her voice got gentle again. "Well, then, let's start at the beginning. How did you think babies got started?"

"I don't know. I can't remember thinking about it much. I guess I'd heard them called gifts from God and little blessings so much—"

"You figured you prayed for them and they came?"

It seemed stupid. Juvenile. "I guess," I said. "Something like that."

"Well, Billie Marie, I think that's pretty. I really do. But it doesn't take into account the babies that come by accident, does it?"

"No." I shook my head. "I knew girls who had babies and weren't married had done something shameful, but I didn't know what. And I never put so much thought into it that I could have explained, but I guess I thought that even God makes mistakes once in a while. He sure seems to have bad aim sometimes, like when somebody good dies young and leaves his kids to grow up poor."

Miss Lydia didn't laugh at me. She looked like she was turning it over in her head. "And that may be as good an explanation as any," she said. "I'd never thought about it being a matter of aim before. But when it comes to babies, there's only one that's ever been born without a little human physical commingling."

I nodded. "I figured that much out recently."

Miss Lydia looked troubled. "Well, what was it that you thought—he—did to you?" We could talk about probably the most personal thing that existed, but she couldn't bring herself to say her son's name.

I halfway yelled, "Well, I didn't think he was trying to give me a baby!" I had known we couldn't have this talk without Curtis coming into it and I'd thought I was ready. I'd been wrong.

"No! No! That's not it at all." She chewed on her lip so hard it started to bleed. "Okay. I see. So there was no reason then for you to make the connection between the two. The . . . intercourse . . . and babies."

"Miss Lydia, what I want to know is why anybody would ever let somebody do that to them even if they wanted a baby real bad. How they could still like them and be nice to them afterward. Why any man who loved his wife would hurt her like that." I had to stop and take a breath.

She took off her glasses and pressed fingers on either side of her nose like she had a headache. When she looked at me again it looked like her heart was broken. I hoped I hadn't done it.

"Lands, child." She stared at an empty chair across the room like she was talking to it. "What was done to you, done to me too, never ever should have happened. It wasn't normal, any more than if a soldier came back from the war and shot his whole family just because once he got killing in his head he couldn't get it out."

"I guess I don't see how there could ever be anything normal about it."

"But you wouldn't, child, that's what I'm saying. In your instance—" She shook her head.

I wasn't sure she was getting my point. "But how can any man want to hurt somebody like that? I mean, if he loves her?"

"Billie Marie." I had never seen Miss Lydia hunt so hard for her words. "There's all kinds of love. And love between a man and a woman, the kind that makes them want to get married, is complicated. I guess one of the ways you know you're in that kind of love is when you— want to do that with him."

"Well then, why not just let him pull off your fingernails one by one with pliers? I guess that'd *really* show him you loved him!" I was getting hot.

"Sugar." She pressed at her tear ducts again. "It's not supposed to hurt. At least not after the first time. And I don't know any more about what's normal for the first time than you do."

"So Mr. Jenkins didn't *make* you let him do that? You *wanted* him to?" I hadn't planned to say that. It came out without warning. She had said we could talk about anything, but this was more than she had bargained for, I'm sure.

She closed her eyes for so long I was afraid she had died of shock. I concentrated until I saw the shallow rise and fall of her chest. When she answered me it was like a voice in a dream.

"Yes, child, I will tell you that I did. And it was then

and only then—when I realized I wanted him to—that I stopped wishing I had died when my daddy . . . had his way."

"Not me," I said. "I'm never gonna want to. I don't care if it means I never get married or have babies or anything. I can't imagine—"

"Oh, but I hope that you will." She raised her head, opened her eyes, and looked at me straight on. "Because that's how you'll know you got over it. That's when you'll know that you're well. Oh, baby child, I do hope that you will."

"Nope," I told her. "You told me I didn't have to get married if I decided not to. Well, if *that's* what it takes to be married, I've already decided."

"No, no, no, no, no, Billie Marie. Listen to me." Miss Lydia's face was clenched into a frown, thinking so hard. I leaned forward in my chair. "You're thinking . . . what was done to you and what goes on between a husband and wife who love each other are one and the same, and they're not. That's like saying . . ." She stared past my shoulder then back into my eyes. ". . . an ostrich and a human being are the same because they've each got two legs." She nodded. "The two have got nothing to do with one another," she went on. "What was done to you . . . *and* me," she reminded, "had nothing to do with love whatsoever. The most you could call it was scratching a filthy itch . . . by a couple of jackasses no better than animals."

I shuddered.

"It's something else entirely when love is in the picture," she said. Her voice lost its hard edge. "Why . . . in those romance novels your mama favors that's what they *call* . . . 'it.' Making love."

Mama had slapped my hand the one time I picked up one of her paperbacks. Now I guessed I knew why.

"Billie Marie, until you can separate the two—what he did to you and what you might do with someone you love—he's still hurting you. And oh, dear child, I do hope someday it'll stop."

I finally told her I understood. That didn't mean I was convinced, though, and I'm sure she knew it.

At least the whole man/woman thing was something I didn't need to worry about just now—and after the days I'd had since St. Swithin's, I could do with a break from worrying. School wasn't even quite so bad without that dark cloud hanging over my head ready to let loose and drown me any minute.

A few days after that talk with Miss Lydia, Harlan fell into step beside me as we were coming in from morning recess. I still felt a little funny playing baseball, but like Harlan had pointed out that first day, it would have been downright stupid to spend all that time alone when they wanted me to play.

And I did enjoy it. Karen and Debbie rolled their eyes at each other for my benefit even more often than usual, but their snottiness had lost most of its sting.

"You must be feeling better," Harlan said.

"Huh?" I hadn't missed a day of school yet.

"Youuu . . . muuuust . . . beeee . . . feeeeeeeliiiiiing . . . betterrrrrrrr." He got right up in my face like ignorant people do when they're talking to a deaf person.

"I heard you. I just don't know what you meant."

"Well, let's see. You've quit beating up your belly like it was full of poison and I haven't seen you crying for, oh, a day or two now."

"Oh." Oh, yeah. I wasn't invisible anymore. "Yeah, I guess I am feeling better."

He started to say something else but Karen and Debbie brushed by just then and knocked my ball glove out of the hand that was swinging at my side. As they passed I heard something about boys and girls and those who were half and half.

"MEOW!" I called at their backs. It was a reflex and I immediately felt stupid for doing it. But by the time they whirled around Harlan was bent double laughing.

"What?" I wasn't sure which of them said it. They were blocking our path, hands on their hips. Tweedledum and Tweedledee Get Indignant. Their makeup looked clownish in the sunlight.

Harlan straightened up and sputtered, "She said 'meow'!" and then convulsed again.

"Meow!" I said to him. It came out like I was thanking him for reminding me. I started laughing myself and then turned to face them. "I said 'meow'! Meow, meow, meow!"

Then I couldn't say it anymore because Harlan and I were both choking and had tears rolling down our cheeks. I was holding my stomach, but I knew he wasn't taking notes now.

"Sounds like you and Harlan have got off on the start of a fun friendship," Miss Lydia commented that evening.

"He is NOT my friend!" I did not understand how any one person could be so bullheaded on a topic. "I study Constitution with him because I have to, and I play baseball with all of them because they want me to and he just happened to think my joke was funny, that's all. . . ." I heard my voice trailing away. The point I was trying to make was no longer clear even to me.

Chapter Twenty-One

A few days later I flew into Miss Lydia's kitchen like usual, splashed a big pile of her mail across the counter, and chattered nonstop for five minutes before I stopped to get my breath and she had a chance to speak.

"How's your mother?" was the first thing she said.

"Huh?"

"Your mother? The woman who lives at your house?" she prodded.

"I don't know. Why?"

"She being nicer to you these days?"

I shrugged. I had been giving Mama about the same amount of attention she gave me—not much more than it took to keep from stepping on her feet. "I guess. My cooking is a lot better these days, thanks to you." I showed her my most wicked grin. "She likes that. Why?"

"Oh well, now, summer's gone and you've got school to tend to. You're even making a friend there, though you won't admit it yet." It was like she was reading me a list she'd made up that day. "Seems to me now that you've gotten the all clear on . . . your health, you know, you won't be needing me for anything anymore."

I couldn't imagine where she might have gotten that idea—it hadn't even crossed my mind. She was at the sink and had turned her back to me. I couldn't see her face. "Miss Lydia. You *are* kidding, aren't you?"

She turned toward me then and I saw she was smiling. But just as I opened my mouth I saw the tiniest speck of uncertainty in her eyes as well. It knocked me back on my heels and I was too stunned to speak for the longest time.

Then I remembered I had worn the ruby heart pin to school that day for the first time just because I woke up so happy. I unpinned it, walked over, and pried her hand open. I laid the pin on her palm and folded her fingers closed around it.

She tried to hand it back. "No, honey! I meant for you to keep that. It's yours."

I put my hands behind me. "How about if it's ours?" I said. "What if whoever needs it most gets to hang onto it for a while?"

She studied me the way a mother memorizes her baby's face. "I do love you, child," she said.

"I love you, too, Miss Lydia. And there's no expiration

date on that. You just remember that."

I was home a couple of hours before Mama and Daddy dragged in and I spent that time thinking how Miss Lydia was slowing down. No doubt about it. Walking cost her more effort all the time. Even changing positions in her chair had become a battle. She and I had started out a woman and a little girl, and we were on our way to trading places just as sure as if we'd bought a ticket.

All I had ever thought about before was how much I needed her.

Chapter Twenty-Two

Harlan and I got so halfway comfortable studying together by mid-October we didn't crawl into opposite corners anymore. One Friday afternoon along about then we were in our usual spot on the stage. I asked him about some Constitution mumbo jumbo, something like which votes require a two-thirds consensus.

He answered me chapter and verse without looking it up and I must have looked surprised. He was miffed.

He said, "Why'd you ask, if you didn't think I knew?"

I said, "It's not that, it's just—" But I didn't know what it was.

"You just don't think I'm very smart." It wasn't a question.

"Oh, Harlan." Truth be told, I had never thought much about him at all. "What do we know about each other, really?" It seemed nicer to flick it off into a generalization and I thought that sounded ever so worldly and grown-up besides.

He huffed, "I know a lot about you."

"Like what?" I said. Name me one person who isn't their own favorite topic of conversation.

He gave me a look. "More than you know about yourself, probably."

Before I could ask him who thought *who* wasn't very smart he looked past me and yelled, "Holy shit!" Then he ran out of the room.

I looked around for what had caused his uproar. I moved to his chair and then it was staring at me. One of those big school wall clocks, reading 4:05.

I found him standing on the front sidewalk looking forlorn. The bus had been gone a good twenty minutes.

He said, "I can't believe nobody came after us."

I said, "Like who?" I mean, neither of us had a best friend to look out for us. And Miss Wilson barely knew where she was most of the time.

Harlan shrugged.

I said, "Well, come on with me, I guess."

He looked at me like I had shot at him. "NO!" He started backing away.

I shook my head. "Harlan, I'm not asking you to run off with me. You're gonna need a phone, aren't you?" I tried the front door of the school. Sure enough, it had locked behind us.

"I can't go home with you!" he protested.

I was a little nervous myself. Then came inspiration. "You don't have to," I said. "I generally take Lydia Jenkins her mail and visit with her for a while. You can come on with me there."

When we got to Miss Lydia's, he looked like he was wound up so tight you could shove a lump of coal up his butt and make a diamond. But if she was surprised to see him it didn't show. "Come in! Come in!" she said. "Good thing I baked cookies today!" Her kitchen smelled like chocolate chip heaven.

I chattered between bites while Harlan shoved whole cookies into his mouth. Miss Lydia stood staring into her sink like she was reading tea leaves. I hadn't noticed the plumber's friend out until she picked it up and started plunging with all her puny might.

Harlan and I both jumped up, but his glare was so fierce I sat back down. Let him have his pride. Boys. After a few grunts he ran some water and shook his head. "Miss Jenkins, you got a crescent wrench?" he said.

"Down in the cellar in an old toolbox," she nodded, "but I won't turn the light on for you unless you call me Miss Lydia."

It took him a minute to realize she was teasing. He

grinned and mumbled, "Okay," while his face turned Easter-egg pink.

He thundered back up with the toolbox and asked for a bucket. I said, "I'll get it." Next I was playing operating room nurse, handing him things and following orders. He had the gooseneck apart, cleaned out, and put back together in less than five minutes.

Miss Lydia sat at the table humming and smiling. When we were done, she told Harlan how nice it was to have somebody come in and take care of a problem like that. He confided that he was quite handy and would be happy to make any number of repairs around the house if she wanted.

My teeth started to ache. My jaw, too. It was killing me to watch them get so chummy in no time flat. I was acting about like a three-year-old forced to share her toys with a visiting cousin, but knowing that didn't change how I felt. I guess I still wasn't sure enough of myself to be sure of Miss Lydia's friendship.

Harlan finally got his mother on the phone and she was there in five minutes flat. Miss Lydia had me get her purse and she started to lay two dollars on him.

I told him not to argue, that he wouldn't win. Then, showing him I was the expert on All Things Lydia I said, "But when she feeds me I make her take a dollar back." So that's what he did.

I moped around in the doorway after he left and said, "I guess I'll go on too." Miss Lydia pressed something into my hand. Small and hard. I knew without looking it was the ruby heart pin. Her Cheshire cat grin made me crack up.

She said, "I know you pretty well, child."

Chapter Twenty-Three

*arlan missed the bus twice the following week and after that he didn't even pretend. His mother finally sat him down and told him she'd rather swing by Cumberland on her way home than worry till he called and then have to make a special trip after him.

She worked for a bookkeeper in Milton and Harlan's youngest older sister had left for junior college that fall. So there was something in this new deal for everybody. Harlan didn't have to rattle around an empty house after school waiting for his mother. She didn't have to worry about him. And Miss Lydia's house got spiffed up better than it had been since Mr. Jenkins died.

As for me, I worked pretty darned hard at deciding Miss Lydia had so much to give there was plenty to share.

So life continued as I had come to know it, with some adjustment. I still went to Miss Lydia's after school, but at least three days a week Harlan was there, too. She treated us both just the same and was so easy to be around.

Harlan started calling me Billie Marie, too, and since it came only from the two of them it fell on my ear like an endearment. Harlan and I stopped being a boy and a girl even at school. We were just two friends.

It was funny. Some of the other kids started acting like we were the cool kids in our class. They'd save us seats at lunch, pick us first for baseball, come show us when they got something new like they were looking for approval. A few, like Karen and Debbie, still thought it was weird for us to hang out together and made sure I knew so, but I didn't care. Maybe that's all "cool" is—not giving a rip what anybody thinks of you.

I hoped Miss Lydia had forgotten about her threat to educate me, but of course she hadn't. Sitting at her kitchen table over brownies and milk late one afternoon, she addressed Harlan. "So. Along about Labor Day, Missy here was already sick of school before it even started . . . and it's no wonder. She says they don't teach you much of anything about the world going on around you. I never heard the like! So I told her I was going to see to it she got a proper education if I had to take the bull by the horns myself." She nodded at me with self-satisfaction and I slid into a glum slouch in my chair. "How about you, Harlan?" she went on. "You have any interest in learning more than who wrote the Monroe Doctrine and who's buried in Grant's Tomb?"

And before I could signal Harlan with my eyes to say "no," he nearly jumped to his feet saying "Yes!" Of course he would. He was nodding so hard it had to hurt. I buried my face in my arms on the table as he went on. "It does get kinda boring being dragged down to the same pace as the slowest kid in the class." He looked at me and I crossed my eyes and stuck out my tongue. He pretended not to see. "And you're right. They don't talk much at all about current events."

Miss Lydia nodded and told him there was a stack of *Time* magazines behind her chair in the living room; would he bring them in, please? She sat humming while he was gone like she was too pleased with herself to notice she was making me miserable.

Harlan came back huffing, carrying a stack of magazines so tall his elbows were straight and his chin rested on top. When he set the pile on the table it spilled every which way and buried the surface in a sea of glossy paper. I thought about that one indecipherable article I'd read about Vietnam and started feeling sick. Even Miss Lydia looked a little overwhelmed. She opened her mouth and then shut it as though she didn't know where to start after all. Some things seem really easy when they're no more than a thought in your head and I figured this was one of those for her.

But just then her grandfather clock chimed five and

it seemed to perk her back up. "Let's go watch the news," she said. "Plenty going on there to talk about." No way was she giving up.

And so we watched the news together and talked about it afterward. Just as we did every day forward that we were there, although after that first day the set didn't come on until 5:30 for Walter Cronkite. Miss Lydia didn't like to watch the Kansas City news—she said she just didn't need to know about *every* baby that was left in a trashcan.

There was more to it than that, but I understood what she meant. Sometimes even the stuff happening halfway around the world seemed too close to home.

She used the back issues of *Time* to look up articles that would help us understand how the current news stories came to be and had them dog-eared and ready when we came after school. We took turns reading out loud and she helped us put the stories in words and terms that we understood. Even the mess in Vietnam started making sense when you took it in small chunks. So did the protests against the mess in Vietnam.

I had never paid attention to what happened before an election for president, but before long Miss Lydia had us talking about all the candidates, Nixon and Humphrey and Wallace, like they were neighbors. She talked about the two-party system and Wallace running as an independent and pointed out articles that explained all the things that could happen with the Electoral College. And there it was, the Constitution we were studying come to life.

She hated George Wallace with such a passion I started expecting her to hiss when he came on the TV. "Children, I would try to let you make up your own minds," she told us, "but I would be derelict if I let you think that man is anything other than the devil in a white shirt and tie." She told us that if he got elected it would "wipe out everything Lyndon Johnson and Reverend King got done and set the United States back a hundred years."

I associated Martin Luther King with marches and protests and riots—and I'd never thought about there being *good* troublemakers in the world. Miss Lydia said if there weren't we'd still be living in a colony and singing "God Save the Queen."

"Yeah, but that's ancient history," I told her.

She looked peeved for a minute. Then she pulled a roll of butcher paper out of a kitchen drawer and tore off a sheet the length of the kitchen table. She had me find a marker and draw a line all the way down the center of the paper, then she started making hash marks across that saying, "Here's the Declaration of Independence. 1776." She made marks for the Civil War, the Great Depression, World Wars I and II and when Harlan and I were born.

Laid out like that it didn't look like such a long span of time and she assured us that it wasn't.

She said, "I know you think I'm older than dirt, but think about your own grandparents and where they fit in with what you learn in your history books. Your time will be in there too, someday." She told us history was nothing more than what happened yesterday.

Neither Harlan nor I knew anyone with a different color skin from our own, so racial issues had never been top of our minds to say the least. But Miss Lydia said all we had to do was listen to one of George Wallace's speeches to know the Civil War wasn't over yet.

She brought us books from the library about Rosa Parks and Reverend King. Then she cut the twine off bales of old *Time* magazines stacked up on the sunporch and looked up articles about the marches on Washington and Montgomery and about lynchings and shootings.

Sometimes it was hard to digest that this was the same world we were living in. Today. It seemed so far away. But then we read about four little girls in Birmingham who went to church one day in 1963 and never came home and we were so ashamed we cried.

One of those afternoons I asked Miss Lydia if there were a lot of colored people in Sedalia when she was growing up.

She frowned. "Some. Why do you ask?"

I shrugged. "I dunno. Mama and Daddy talk about the colored like they're scared of them or something. I was just wondering how you got to think the way you do."

She was standing at the kitchen sink and her weight slumped against the counter while she stared out the window a long minute. Then she said, "There on that timeline, the year after the Civil War ended, my daddy was born. *His* daddy fought that war. Fought for the side of the South."

She took her glasses off and polished them on her apron. Buying time to shop for words. "As a child, Billie Marie, I heard him tell stories that made my stomach churn," she said. "Granddaddy liked to call himself a religious man, but I didn't know how to come home from church and reconcile myself to the things some folks thought they had a right to do to other people. Flesh and blood. Men, women, and children—pieces of property and not treated with the kindness you'd show a dog." She bit her lip and said, "There is a kind of man in the world that gets meanness confused with power and I still can't reconcile that."

She wasn't talking just about her granddaddy. I knew. That day in July she had told me there was something wrong with the men on that side of the family and called herself worse than Typhoid Mary for passing it on.

And I understood that part of what she was teaching Harlan and me—and why—was to make up for it.

School itself was still a joke but at least now it was one I shared. Harlan and I breezed through our class work. Then we read the biographies and novels Miss Lydia brought us from town. If it was a book she hadn't read she asked us to work together on a report and pretended it was so she could learn too, but I knew it was mainly to get us to discuss and decide what was important.

She read everything we wrote and prodded us to go just a little bit farther with everything we studied. It wasn't enough to tell her the who, what, and when. She asked for the why—and if that was impossible to know, she asked for our thoughts on the matter. Harlan and I learned to argue without getting mad, and it practically became a hobby.

That woman had a knack for asking the one question that could nail you to the spot and make you question everything you thought you'd decided. If we said the demonstrators at the 1968 Chicago Democratic convention were unpatriotic, she asked us which parts of the First Amendment we'd keep and what we'd throw out. If we hollered "police brutality" against any of the protestors anywhere, she asked us to define at what specific moment and with what qualification a demonstration becomes a riot. She made us look at both sides of everything.

Just like when she'd figured out how to teach me to crochet, she was a natural.

I was learning a lot from Harlan and Miss Lydia that didn't come from books, too. I learned more about kindness than I ever had at church. Kindness and generosity.

Harlan's mom turned forty-five that February and he and his sisters planned a surprise party. The youngest girl was off at college and the older two were married with little kids and lived at least sixty miles away, so it was hard for the whole family to get together anymore, sometimes even for Christmas. This party was a month in the planning.

Harlan's dad pitched in by getting Mrs. Willits out of the house that Saturday afternoon. When Harlan got his film developed, he showed me the picture he took right when his mother walked in and saw the decorations and all her little chicks home to roost. It made me cry. I had never seen such pure joy. I didn't know you could take a picture of love. For me it was like peeking through a window at a different way to live.

When school let out that spring, I was lost. It wasn't the same anymore with just Miss Lydia and me day after day. It was like feeling phantom pain from an amputated limb.

And I know it was hard on Harlan. Neither he nor I had been big phone talkers up until that point, but we started logging at least half an hour on the telephone with each other every day.

Then he showed up at Miss Lydia's one day toward the end of June in a dilapidated old pickup. A big grin smeared across his face. I was so happy I couldn't stop wiggling.

Harlan was one boy who didn't have to ride a tractor every spare minute—his folks had both inherited a fair bit of land and that gave his dad the luxury of hiring outside help. But Harlan did have chores—mainly tending the five or so kinds of animals they always had around the homestead waiting to become dinner. He told us he hadn't been able to get done every morning in time to ride with his mother on her schedule.

But his father had decided he could drive the five miles into Cumberland and back as long as he kept to dirt roads and only came for the afternoons. Mr. Willits was afraid all the work Harlan had done for Miss Lydia would come undone over a summer of neglect.

Right.

Harlan's folks were about as kind and decent as they come. I barely knew them directly—they didn't belong to our church, so I only saw them at school programs or the occasional funeral—but I'd heard Harlan's stories. And I knew what kind of boy they'd turned out.

We spent most of that summer cleaning Miss Lydia's house top to bottom, inside and out. We took down curtains and rehung them washed and pressed after the windows were clean. We beat rugs over the clothesline until we were choking on dust. We polished furniture. We scrubbed floors on our knees and then waxed them until we could see our reflections.

For her part Miss Lydia ran the best restaurant in town, open anytime we got hungry. And she still insisted on paying us a dollar a day.

Mostly we took a break from studying—but sometimes we couldn't help getting caught up in what was going on. On July 16 Harlan came early to watch Apollo 11 lift off live on TV. We had seen rocket ships take off before, but this was a much, much bigger deal.

Four days later we parked ourselves in front of Miss Lydia's TV at noon and by the time 3:18 rolled around and Neil Armstrong told us "The *Eagle* has landed," my butt muscles were sore from being clenched. We could hear the cheering of the men at Houston Control, but Harlan's watch ticking was the only sound in that room with the three of us.

We listened all afternoon while Walter Cronkite and Wally Schirra explained what was going on and sometimes we heard the conversation between the moon—the moon!—and Houston. All three of us were afraid we'd miss something if we so much as went to the bathroom.

I didn't know how they could get the TV picture to us from space, but Miss Lydia explained about satellites and signals and made me understand about as well as I understood how music came out of the radio. Then she took off her glasses and dabbed at her eyes and I asked her what was wrong.

"Nothing, child," she said. "I just never thought I'd live to see the day."

"Why not?" I asked her. "This space race thing has been going on since way back when Kennedy was president. You told us yourself."

Miss Lydia chuckled, but not like she was laughing at me. "Billie Marie, you got to realize," she said, "when I was your age I rode a mule to school. Only the richest men owned automobiles, and even they still called them 'horseless carriages.' You and Harlan here"—he tore his eyes away from the screen to listen—"will never have to worry about polio, but you're just about the first crop that didn't. That's a fear I lived with most of my life." She wiped her eyes again with the back of a wrist. "Now here I sit with cars buzzing up and down the street, thousands of people traveling by airplane over the country at this very minute, and I'm about to watch a man walk on the moon. It's almost too much to take in."

Harlan and I looked at each other and I wondered if my eyes were opened as wide as his.

He called his mom when he knew she'd be home from work and asked if he could stay late. He had pulled the phone cord all the way into the living room next to me so I heard when she said, "Well . . . let me talk to Miss Jenkins, would you?"

The phone wouldn't reach so I helped Miss Lydia hoist up out of her chair and take a few stiff steps toward the kitchen. "Hello," she said, then, "Uh-huh. Uh-huh. I think that's a fine idea. No, no, don't worry. It's just fine."

She handed the phone back to Harlan and I heard his mother say "Behave yourself. I love you" and Harlan said, "I love you, too, Mom."

It sounded so normal. I was amazed.

Harlan hung up and raised his eyebrows at Miss Lydia. "Your mama asked if I'd kick your butt out early enough in the morning to go do your chores," she told him. "I promised her I would. So settle in. You're staying the night."

I stewed and squirmed until my folks pulled into their driveway about nine, and I called as soon as they were in the house. Daddy answered and I talked way too fast. "They're just about to walk on the moon and we've been watching all afternoon and please can I stay? Please?"

I heard him sigh. He said in a tired voice, "Ten o'clock."

"Oh, but Daddy I don't know how much more there'll be and it's not like there's school tomorrow—"

"I said 'ten o'clock.'" No louder, no edge. No room for bargaining, either. I told him okay.

A few minutes later none of us blinked as that grainy gray guy in the fat space suit bounced down those steps. Neil Armstrong's "one small step for man, one giant leap for mankind" fell on us like a prayer. We helped Miss Lydia up when "The Star-Spangled Banner" started and we were all three standing there bawling by the end. We knew each other's minds well enough by then not to bother feeling stupid about it.

Out in the middle of nowhere, we were connected by live television transmission to the brotherhood of man. And in that one little room the three of us were connected to one another by something even stronger than blood.

At ten o'clock Miss Lydia followed me to the door and asked in a low voice, "You have the ruby pin these days, right?" I nodded and she said, "Do me a favor and pin it to your nightgown tonight." She pinched my cheek and I managed a smile as she closed the door with Harlan on her side of it.

Our house was dark and my parents were in bed when I let myself in. I walked through the living room and put my hand on top of the TV. It was cold.

I knew my parents had to work hard. But it seemed to me just then they could make time to look up if they wanted to. If not at me, at least. At the world outside.

For the first time, I felt sorry for them that they weren't me.

Chapter Twenty-Four

*I*t couldn't be avoided forever. By early August we had cleaned every inch of Miss Lydia's house except behind that one closed door and there was just no plausible explanation to give Harlan for wanting to skip it. Besides, I figured it would have to be dealt with someday, and better us than Miss Lydia.

I had myself believing it wouldn't bother me. But as soon as I stepped inside, it *smelled* like Curtis. All sweat and cigarette smoke. It was over ninety degrees in there and I started shaking like a barefoot Christmas caroler.

Harlan asked what was wrong. I couldn't look at him. I kept trying to clear my throat but couldn't get past a phlegmy gargling sound. Sweat started running out of my hairline into my eyes and even so I was shaking hard enough to rattle my teeth. The smell of the room turned into a taste in my mouth.

Harlan asked if I was getting sick. I shook my head. Then I reconsidered and shrugged. I reached back to steady myself against the headboard of the bed then pulled my hand away like I'd been burned.

I could see Harlan out of the corner of my eye. He bowed his head and clasped his hands down low in front the way men pray at church.

Without saying anything more, he took me by the shoulders and propelled me out of the room and down the stairs. Miss Lydia was in her chair in the front room staring at a television that wasn't turned on.

Harlan steered me to the end of the sofa nearest her chair. He walked to the doorway and looked back and forth between the two of us half a dozen times, studying us for what seemed like an hour. He spent some time after that studying his shoes.

Then he said, "You know, Miss Lydia, it's such a pretty day it's a shame for us all to be inside. You keep saying your iris bed needs to be thinned out and I know my mom would love to have some. Could you maybe show Billie Marie where to dig?"

I don't believe in love at first sight. It might make for an easy shortcut if somebody's writing a movie, but in real life I think it's nothing more than hormones performing a parlor trick. I have come to believe that real love is like learning to read, one letter at a time, sounding things out until it all comes together. It takes time to build, step after step. And I know that was the exact moment Harlan climbed up that first step for me.

He must have worked like a dervish, because he was finished by our usual parting time. The bed of his old pickup was filled with plastic garbage bags. You could smell a mix of pine cleaner and Glade wafting down the stairs.

He said, "Miss Lydia, unless you've got other plans, I'll just take all those bags of clothes home and have Mom drop them off at Goodwill tomorrow."

She had to clear her throat to mumble, "You're a good one, son."

I did the same before whispering, "Yeah. Yeah, you sure are."

It was impossible to tell whether he was happy or horrified. He turned beet-purple, nodded, and left.

That night, Curtis raped me over and over again in my dreams. I would wake up drenched in sweat. Feeling actual pain. It would take forever to calm down and get back to sleep.

Then my head would hit that lunchroom floor and it would start all over.

About the fourth or fifth time, just before Curtis could wrestle my panties off, Harlan came running into the lunchroom with a big gun and chased Curtis off.

You don't have to be Freud to figure that one out.

Miss Lydia looked almost as haggard as me the next

day and I figured her night hadn't been any better. Harlan showed up with a guitar—I hadn't even known he played—and after lunch he insisted we sing all the songs we knew. Even "The Itsy-Bitsy Spider" and baby stuff like that. Before we knew it Miss Lydia and I were laughing our heads off.

He was starting to flat-out astound me.

Chapter Twenty-Five

*G*oing back to school in September was barely a bump in the road. I didn't look forward to it like Christmas, but there was no reason to dread it either.

KarenDebbie came back to seventh grade with their skirts even shorter, makeup even thicker, and their hair bleached to a brassy gold. They looked uneasy when they said hello to me and I couldn't tell if they were unsure of themselves or me. I didn't care. I could barely believe I had ever thought they mattered.

The boys in our class all came back about three inches taller. Their faces had erupted in angry pimples. They bounced off the walls like Labrador puppies—it was almost like somebody had put something in their water.

The eighth-grade girls huddled and giggled and kept to themselves—other than trying to distract the eighth-grade boys from staring at KarenDebbie.

Harlan had spent the last two weeks at home helping his mother, so it had been that long since I had seen him.

Mrs. Willits planted a gigantic garden every year, probably an idea left over from having four kids at home, and she had taken time away from her job late August to fill the pantries and freezers.

When I laid eyes on Harlan that day he looked like he'd grown an inch. His face was starting to sprout fuzz but his skin was clear. Amid those other train wrecks he looked handsome. But when you care about somebody it seems like they automatically gain about twenty points in the looks department. Maybe he was plain as ever and I just couldn't see it anymore.

Our teacher, a Mr. Landis, didn't look old enough to be out of high school. Ten minutes after the bell rang we knew his deal. He had graduated college the spring before with a degree in economics. The only reason he had applied for this job was to stay out of the draft.

Harlan and I exchanged a look that said we were going to be on our own another year.

Now we had twice-a-day study hour instead of recess. Mr. Landis said he wanted us to keep our Constitution study partners from the year before and use one of those hours for extra concentrated work. It was starting to look like Cumberland C. P. was under a lot of pressure to have us pass that test at year's end. There must have been government money involved for them to care so much.

Harlan raised his hand and asked if we could use both study hours every day if we thought we needed them. Mr. Landis said that would be fine. It took extra-concentrated work on my part not to laugh.

Miss Lydia called her own school to session the same week the bogus real one started and announced that, besides the day-to-day news, we were going to focus on the women's movement, women's lib.

I was thoroughly and utterly appalled—the conversations I'd overheard at home about hairy-legged bra burners were even more acid than those about colored people. I hadn't formed an independent opinion of my own yet, but I knew without any consideration whatsoever that I didn't want to be discussing bras around Harlan. *Or* any body parts that needed shaving.

I said, "No, Miss Lydia, you can't just decide that. I, for one, won't do it!" and felt darned proud I was confident enough to put my foot down.

She shot me a look so hot I could almost smell my hair burning. It caught me by surprise, to say the least. I took a step back and, by reflex, put up my hands and said, "Hey, okay! Don't shoot! I'm sorry!"

She blinked a couple of times and then broke out laughing. I was staring at my bedroom ceiling later that night before I realized just what I'd said.

I was so mortified I decided I couldn't even bring it

up to apologize. Harlan hadn't said anything, but it was hard to know if it hadn't kicked him in the gut or if he was too decent to say so.

I went back the next afternoon a most eager and willing pupil in the subject of women's lib.

I hadn't kept up with all the news that summer but now there were almost as many women's demonstrations and marches on TV as there were protests against the Vietnam War. I had to admit it was a current event hard to ignore.

But I still wasn't sure I could discuss all the issues— birth control and abortion and such—with Harlan in the mix. I tried to squirm off the hook by saying he couldn't possibly be interested.

He looked at me with those big blue eyes that looked darker every day and said, "You think I don't care about my sisters? You think I don't care what happens to you?"

I think I melted some just about then.

It turned out there was plenty to go around when it came to making us uncomfortable. First off, it felt a lot more personal than when we were studying civil rights. Then we had been reading about people who were very different from us in places far away. They had problems we personally would never have to face.

But there was no way to remove our own families from discussions about the roles men and women play. It was a subject that knocked on everybody's door, that walked right on into everybody's house no matter who they were.

It set us talking about everyone we knew. A lot of the wives worked now, and that seemed like a fairly recent development once it came up for consideration. But none of us knew of a single man who cooked or cleaned. Not before their wives worked, not since. Talking about it out loud made me feel like a Peeping Tom.

Harlan started out, instinct I suppose, trying to defend the men. But even he couldn't come up with a convincing case once he really thought about it. Like a lot of things, it had seemed normal until there was reason to question it. He was left feeling off balance too.

And all of it kept bringing me back to Mama. She wasn't the only woman who worked, but she was the only one around who did a man's work driving tractors. I pondered for hours on end how she and Daddy had ever come to *that* agreement. And whether or not it had been completely mutual.

She had mentioned dancing and dining with Daddy years before at the Savoy Grille. But somewhere down the road they had evolved into what appeared to be business partners. I thought about those romance novels Mama read and wondered just how far away she was living from her idea of happily ever after.

And I wondered if pure instinct had showed her the safest place to put the blame was on my head.

None of these explanations would make the way she treated me fair. None of them would make it right. But from what I was figuring out about human nature and Mama's view of the world, those explanations would make sense.

Finally the notion started sinking in just how disappointed a woman would have to be to name her daughter William, too stricken to even move on and choose another name. How, beyond farmwork, a son would have also been more valuable to someone like Mama because of his potential to grow up into a big deal that would earn her bragging rights.

The idea would never occur to Mama that I could become a big deal. Or that she could, for that matter.

Miss Lydia introduced Harlan and me to the fact that a women's movement was nothing new and took us back to talk about the founding fathers. I guess she knew it was time to stop us from picking apart every family we knew.

She said that back when the Continental Congress was framing the Constitution, Abigail Adams told her husband John not to forget the ladies, "but that's exactly what the lot of them did. They gave the women no rights whatsoever. They couldn't even own land."

"But that's why the men were trying to break from

England in the first place," Harlan pointed out. "Taxation without representation—they had no say in their own government."

Miss Lydia nodded and we chewed on that a good long while.

It was clear she had done homework of her own. She told us it was four years after the Civil War that Susan B. Anthony and Elizabeth Stanton began working toward an amendment that would give women the right to vote. She made sure we knew just how hard they had to fight.

There it was, in our faces again: the Constitution.

She had us read about a march down Pennsylvania Avenue on Woodrow Wilson's Inauguration Day in 1913 and how it turned ugly. How the police were called in and hundreds of women wound up in the hospital.

It made the hairs on the back of my neck stand up. "Just like Washington this time," I said. "Montgomery, too."

And Miss Lydia assured us that no matter who it was—revolutionaries, the colored, women, whoever—nobody would stay down forever without rising up. Without fighting back. She was looking me square in the eye when she said it.

I nodded that I understood.

When we'd worked up to 1920 and the Nineteenth Amendment, Miss Lydia put the candle on the cake, so to speak. "And that, children," she said, "is how I came to be among the first women in the United States to cast a vote for president."

Harlan's mouth gaped as wide as mine. She'd told us before to put our grandparents in the timeline of the history we studied, but we had forgotten. Of course Miss Lydia was born before the turn of the twentieth century. What she was teaching us had started as a current event for her.

That was early spring before planting season so Mama was home and cooking dinner when I got home. I was so excited about what I'd just learned I sat down at the table and told her all about it. ". . . and Miss Lydia says that's all history is, today looking back at yesterday."

"Miss Lydia says too many things," Mama snapped. The edge on her voice stung like a slap to the face.

She was moving between the kitchen cabinet and the stove slamming pots and lids around as she went. I had been too caught up in my story to notice her bad mood hanging over the room like a cloud.

"I'm sorry." My mouth formed the words out of habit. "I . . . guess I do talk about her a lot." The words came slowly, but my mind was starting to spin.

When I dare talk to you at all, is what I thought. When I've taken your temperature and calculated the weight of the air in the room and decided it's safe to have you notice me. When I'm saying anything at all to you other than "I'm sorry."

Anger built inside me like steam and a cool mustache of sweat broke out on my upper lip. Things began to swim until Mama became nothing but a blur.

And then, all at once, it was right there in front of me. All of it. All the times she ignored me and all the criticism when she didn't. All the times I thought she didn't love me and blamed myself because my best wasn't good enough for her. All the times I'd felt guilty just for being born.

All the time I'd spent putting out little brush fires everywhere when really it was the whole forest that was ablaze. In a haze, I saw it all.

And as soon as I could name it, it was gone. The anger dissipated so suddenly I was left feeling light-headed. Eye of the storm.

Before I even knew it was coming I said, "I feel sorry for you, Mama."

She whirled around and dripped soup from a ladle onto the floor without noticing. "What did you just say?"

My pulse didn't even quicken. I almost laughed. "I said, 'I feel sorry for you.'" Our eyes locked and the soup boiled over on the stove without either of us moving to save it.

"What . . . do you mean . . . by that?" She had no idea what had just passed through me.

"I feel sorry for you because I've got Miss Lydia and

you're not that close to anybody." I just stated it as fact. "And it's your own fault." I chuckled. "You sure couldn't get close to me with your son standing in the way."

She snorted. "I don't know what the hell you're talking about and you don't either."

"The fourth member of this family," I told her. "You know. The kid you wanted. The one you didn't have. I get the feeling you've always spent more time thinking about him than you did me. I'm just the one you got stuck with."

She looked like I had kicked her. "Why I ought to—," she started.

"Oh, save it, Mama," I sighed. "I really don't care anymore." I recognized it as truth when I heard it. She was slack jawed and blinking when I turned to go to my room.

Later I heard the TV go on and went to the kitchen to fix myself a bowl of soup with plenty of crackers on the side. Daddy looked up from the table and asked, "Do you know what's wrong with your mother?"

I told him yes and left the room without explaining.

I stood by her in the living room until she looked up from her book. I took a deep breath and said, "I'm sorry. I hurt your feelings and I shouldn't have." It was a long way from taking back what I'd said—and that fact hung in the air between us.

She said, "Oh, I guess we both say things sometimes we don't mean." Fishing.

"Okay, then," I told her. "I've got homework to do while I eat." I went to my room and shut her out.

We took the U.S. Constitution test the first week of May 1970. It was the same week the National Guard shot and killed four students at Kent State University in Ohio while they were exercising their rights as guaranteed by the First Amendment. As far as I know, Harlan and I were the only seventh graders in Cumberland who recognized that horrible parallel.

We did well enough to bring the class average up to "acceptable" on the government table of scores. Mr. Landis was so grateful that we knew eighth grade would be a free ride to do pretty much what we pleased.

You get to know a teacher by the end of that first year with them. From dodging the draft to celebrating "acceptable," we knew he didn't care about much more than covering his own bacon.

Chapter Twenty-Six

Harlan and I spent June scraping and priming Miss Lydia's house and the rest of the summer painting. We three had powwowed as soon as warm weather hit and decided on the project and assignments.

Harlan's job was to work on the weatherboard siding of the house.

My job was to do all the trim work—windows and doors.

Miss Lydia's job was to buy the supplies, keep us fueled with home cooking, and sit inside whichever window I was working on and keep me company.

She made sure the Willitses knew how grateful she was for Harlan's help and she gave Mama a call whenever it was time to make her Queen for a Day. But truth was, she and Harlan and I were the real family by then. It just felt like we all belonged to one another.

We could talk about anything. Or nothing. We could finish each other's sentences and we did. And while I know the ruby pin passed back and forth a few times and Harlan went home in a minor snit more than once, I came to see that's bound to happen when any three people spend as much time together as we did and I learned it wasn't the end of the world. Almost nothing we got into it about was important enough that I remember it now. Except for one time, nothing came between us that couldn't be fixed by a pan of Miss Lydia's apple dumplings.

The day I did the window trim on Curtis's room while Miss Lydia sat inside, I thought we did a great job of playing normal. But I guess we all knew each other better than that. End of the day, Harlan called me over by his truck after Miss Lydia shut the front door.

He looked into my eyes and said, "It was him, wasn't it?"

I said, "What are you talking about?" but my face was already on fire.

Harlan said, "It was Miss Lydia's son that hurt you." It wasn't a question this time.

"I have no idea what you mean." My knees felt weak and, even so, I wanted to run.

He spat into the dust by his feet and squinted at the horizon. "Billie Marie," he said, "you came back to school sixth grade wounded as a wing-shot bird. *Something* had happened and I'm pretty sure I know what it was."

Don't cry. Don't cry. I had thought it out so many

times—if somebody figured out anything, they'd figure out everything. Fear I hadn't felt in nearly two years started twisting me up.

Harlan said, "It's okay. You don't have to tell me."

Then the tears started rolling.

He went on, "But I hope someday you want to."

I nodded and busted full-out sobbing. He put his arms around me—the first time he ever touched me on purpose—and cradled my head on his shoulder.

We stood like that a long time. I could feel Miss Lydia looking at us through a window but I didn't turn to see.

Chapter Twenty-Seven

*I*t's not that nothing happened in the next two-and-a-half years. Days do follow one another without a single one of them being empty. But life as I had come to know it had been going on long enough it was like singing the same song with only an occasional new verse.

Harlan and I breezed through eighth grade about as we had expected. We scored so high on all the standard tests Miss Mitchell, the principal herself, called us in to thank us. I got the impression we were practically all that was keeping the tax money coming.

Not that we were that smart. I have no false pride in that regard. But we didn't depend on the school. Miss Lydia pushed us and we pushed each other. We read and discussed stuff every day.

Miss Lydia got the idea from a TV quiz show to make up a stack of flash cards and then she added to them every week. Every so often we'd have our own contest.

She'd hold up a card that said JANUARY 30, 1968 and

Harlan and I would race to yell, "Tet Offensive!"

It would say "SALT" and we'd trip over our tongues saying, "Strategic Arms Limitation Treaty." It was really hard jumping from one subject to another like that but making it a competition made us try harder. I'm sure Miss Lydia had known that it would.

One game, half an hour in, she held up a card that said "LBJ." Harlan and I gave each other a "what the—?" look before we both shouted, "Lyndon Baines Johnson!"

Miss Lydia shook her head and I thought oh, I see. "Lady Bird Johnson!" I said.

She shook her head again.

Harlan took a stab. "Lynda Bird Johnson?"

Nope. It took me several seconds to come up with "Luci Baines Johnson?"

That still wasn't it. Harlan and I frowned, stumped.

"Lydia Belle Jenkins," she said primly and went on to the next card before we'd stopped laughing.

The other students at school seemed like sleepwalkers except when hormones cattle-prodded somebody into doing something impressively stupid. The seventh-grade side of the room was half-empty for a week's suspension after Sherry Day collected a dollar from every boy who wanted to take a peek inside her bloomers and then made good on the deal after lunch in the upstairs hallway.

But most of the time it was like dancing in a building full of plodding zombies.

Harlan and I were still the only mixed pair of best friends. But by then nobody seemed to think anything of it at all.

That happens in a small town. Somebody passing through might stop at the grain elevator for a cold drink and be shocked to see an old man feeding his lap dog every other bite of his sandwich, but a local would just say, "Oh, that's old man Sullivan. He's always been sweet on his little dogs."

I guess it's easier to live in a fishbowl if you just decide to accept the stripes on the other fish.

Then there was the matter of Mama. I don't know if calling her bluff had awakened a conscience in her or if she just didn't find it as much fun to get mad and rear up at someone who didn't care. But she had gotten a whole lot tamer and sometimes it even seemed like we had traded places and she was trying to get in good with me.

A couple of times she asked if I'd like to go along to town with her on Saturday—and I told her "no, thank you." She moved us all back to the kitchen table for dinner and, for a few evenings, asked me just what we were studying at school. I gave her the shortest possible answer and added, "Thanks for asking, Mama," each time. I was ever so polite. A week later she went back to eating in the living room.

We weren't any chummier than ever, but just the lack of yelling—and not living on edge waiting for the next firestorm—made for a happier house.

Even Daddy was happier. I guess. I still didn't know much about what Daddy thought other than how everybody was out to get Nixon and the way the goddamned government is always trying to keep the farmer down. That, and he usually had an opinion about whether or not it was going to rain.

But his face wasn't set in a permanent frown anymore. I took that as a step in the direction of happy, anyway.

Ninth grade I went back to school wearing a little mascara and lip gloss. Harlan didn't say anything, but he did start opening doors for me. The second day at lunch I caught a faint whiff of something new. I sneaked looks until I saw evidence he had started shaving.

It was funny to have so many things about us changing while everything else stayed exactly the same. Funny peculiar, that is.

We had exchanged small gifts for birthdays and Christmas two years running. Miss Lydia always gave Harlan and me each a book, I crocheted some little something for her, and by then Harlan had a homemade birdhouse hanging on every branch outside her house that would hold one. For one another, Harlan and I usually bought music albums—something to share.

But that year I gave Harlan a George Carlin album and he gave me tiny ruby heart earrings. We were on the stage during study hour. I opened the little velvet box and was so surprised I just said, "Oh!"

Harlan said, "To go with your pin." He sounded pretty proud. Of course he knew about the ruby pin that passed between Miss Lydia and me. There had even been times one of us had stuck our foot in our mouth and he'd defused the situation with a world-weary voice saying, "Oookay. Which one of you has the pin?"

When I saw those earrings I was so embarrassed I tried to make a joke—"Well, gee, Harlan, does this mean you're going to pierce your ears so we can pass these back and forth?"

It was absolutely the wrong thing to say and I was sorry that instant. He looked more disappointed than angry, but he walked out and didn't speak to me anymore that day.

The next day Christmas break started, and four days running he refused to come to the phone when I called. I cried and shut myself up in my room and wrote him letters that I tore up. I told Miss Lydia the whole story and threw myself on her mercy for advice.

"You'll sort it out, I expect," was all she would say. But I could tell it bothered her too.

Christmas morning I answered the phone and heard his flat "Hi."

I started blubbering—"Oh, Harlan, I'm so sorry, I didn't mean—" but he interrupted.

"What time are we having Christmas with Miss Lydia?" he said. He was trying to sound cold but couldn't quite pull it off.

I felt twenty pounds lighter. I said, "Well, we're going over at noon. She insisted on cooking. Why don't you come, too? You know she'll have enough for twenty people."

"Naw," he said. "Mom's cooking too and the girls are all home this year. We got aunts and uncles and cousins coming out our ears . . . probably four o'clock is about the earliest I can sneak away."

"I'll tell Miss Lydia," I said, "and I'm sure she'll be fine with that. Oh, and Harlan?" I added. "Merry Christmas."

There was only the least pause before he said, "Merry Christmas to you too." I felt all fuzzy inside.

Chapter Twenty-Eight

When I was fifteen, Miss Lydia was closing in on eighty. She had gradually done more spectating and less participating when we worked around her house, but Harlan and I noticed her really starting to slip. She forgot things. It was so hard to get up and down she quit doing it very often.

Come summer I started taking her mail over at eleven instead of noon, making the excuse that I wanted to visit with her alone before Harlan got there. Really it was so I could help her cook. She never let on but I knew she was grateful.

We were caught up with all the big projects by then. We had tilled and fertilized her garden, pruned her shrubs, reseeded her lawn, done everything we could think of. We did another major cleaning job inside, but it only took a fourth the time as before.

So we started to just spend time with her visiting. It seemed like what she needed most. We asked questions and let her tell all her stories, even the ones we had heard before. She brought her brothers and her Avery back to life one story at a time. We got to see glimpses of her as a girl in the shine of her eyes.

One day I went to put one of her picture albums back in the dresser upstairs and just as I started to close the drawer I saw something under the edge of the liner paper. I pulled out two pictures that had been lying loose. The one on top looked like Curtis and some woman his age, but the picture was way too old. I stared. It had to be.

I flipped the picture over. "Evie Lee and Haney Sanders, 1901" was written on the back. Miss Lydia's parents.

I looked at the second picture. Still Curtis, I'd testify in court. I felt cold all of a sudden.

Every time Miss Lydia had looked at her grown son she had seen the face of her daddy. The man who was supposed to protect her and didn't.

She hadn't killed just Curtis that night. She had killed the man who hurt her too. A little worm of guilt I hadn't even realized lived within me sprouted wings and flew away.

I tore the pictures into tiny pieces and flushed them down the upstairs commode. Miss Lydia wouldn't want to visit them again, I knew, and neither would I. Nobody else needed to know. As the water swirled them away I whispered, "Amen." Then I scrubbed my hands in water a lot hotter than it really needed to be.

When I went downstairs I could see the child inside that old woman's failing body and I wanted to take her on my lap and rock her like a baby.

Not that she had gone all soft or feeble-minded. She'd threaten to whip us if we tried to do more for her than she wanted. She was kidding, of course—but we were half-convinced she could. She was still in charge, no doubt about it.

But it was clear she wasn't going to be leading any more crusades for higher knowledge. Any more debates on world events. She'd get the flashcards out every once in a while, I think mainly to reassure herself, but she wasn't making up any new ones and the magazines piled up beside her chair unread.

I knew she couldn't concentrate long enough to read long articles. She lost the thread of our conversation so often I learned the look that came into her eyes and I'd change the subject. She had always allowed me my dignity even though I was just a kid. The least I could do was return the favor.

Sometimes after lunch she would fall asleep in her chair while Harlan and I did the dishes. We took those opportunities for Harlan to give me driving lessons.

When I turned sixteen in November, Miss Lydia

baked an angel food cake from scratch. It was so light that every bite was like snapping at the wind. But her birthday surprise came the week I got my driver's license.

She had asked Mama to take her to Milton that Saturday, and that morning she asked if I would go along too. Mama waited for me to say, "No, thank you," and a little cloud passed over her face when I didn't. But she did hold her tongue.

We got to town and Miss Lydia asked Mama to drive her to the Walsner-Fusz car dealership. And Mama sat at the Fourth and Main stop sign until the car behind her laid on the horn. Then she pulled away about one mile an hour like she was moving under protest and said, "Lydia, you are *not* buying that girl a car. I won't have it."

Miss Lydia stared straight ahead, hands crossed atop the pocketbook in her lap. "I'm not. I'm buying one for myself."

Mama gave her a "don't bullshit me" look. I know it well. It's deadly.

Miss Lydia pointed her chin at the windshield. "Might be just what I need to attract a boyfriend."

I about blew my brains out my ears trying to hold back *that* laugh. Even Mama couldn't last more than three seconds. We all laughed our way to Walsner-Fusz.

Eugene Walsner first tried to talk Miss Lydia into a new car instead of used, saying she'd just be buying someone else's problems. She fixed him with a steady look and said, "Eugene, are you saying you've got a whole lot full of problems out there for sale, but you're going to do *me* the favor of not selling me one?" And he blustered and blushed and started showing her around the used car lot.

Mama and I trailed them and Mama weighed in with as many opinions as Mr. Walsner. Talking at the same time, it was hard to understand either of them. But Miss Lydia took her time and nodded every so often, walking around cars and occasionally looking up at me. I didn't know what she wanted from me but I guess she found it when we got to the Cadillac DeVille sitting back in the corner. It was a 1965 but its mermaid-green paint job looked brand new and, at least to me, it looked more like a jewel than a car. Miss Lydia took one look at my face and smiled.

She asked Mr. Walsner to take her for a test drive in it but he was already on to the next car, a 1970 Ford, telling her how it was better suited to her needs. "Do you always argue your customers out of what they want?" she asked and he went inside for the keys.

Mama and I rode in the back seat while Mr. Walsner drove around three blocks and came back. He parked on the street in front of the showroom and Miss Lydia turned to me and nodded.

We all went inside and the negotiations began. Mr. Walsner started out asking $1800 and it was a long, hard road down to the $1450 they finally settled on. Along the way he told Miss Lydia, among other things, that she was a real good horse trader and she told him he reminded her of one specific part of a horse. He had big sweat rings on his blue shirt and no doubt believed he had earned every one-hundred-dollar bill she counted out on the counter. And then some.

He threw a "Come back again!" at our backs that sounded like it was automatic.

Miss Lydia turned and fixed a look on him that took another inch off his height. "If I *ever* find myself in need of another car," she said, "you'll be hearing from me, all right."

"Yes, ma'am." He knew she wasn't talking about the prospect of another sale down the road. You could see his Adam's apple bobbing up and down.

I drove Miss Lydia home in that land yacht with the Cadillac emblem on the hood and felt like we were flying. The only thing I had ever driven was the Willitses' old beater of a pickup and compared to that I was chauffeur to the queen.

I did hope I would never have to parallel park the thing. Even the steering wheel was so big it felt like I was playing grown-up. Miss Lydia kept looking out the side window.

I'm pretty sure she couldn't see over the dashboard.

I knew better than to tell her she shouldn't have bought it. I just pulled up into her driveway where Mr. Jenkins used to park and handed her the key. She nodded, pleased with herself, and started the long haul out.

She had one foot on the ground when I got to her and I did more lifting than steadying to get her on her feet. She had been getting smaller while I kept growing. By then I was a head taller than her and probably outweighed her by fifteen pounds.

She rested before starting for the house, then said, "You run on. I expect your mama's got up a full head of steam by now. When she gets through bawling you out for what you didn't do, come on back. I have something."

But Mama didn't say a word about the car while I helped her carry in groceries. While we were putting things away, I got it. She wasn't saying anything at all. The whole car affair had knocked her nose out of joint. She threw me a look when I told her Miss Lydia needed me for a while. I shrugged it off as soon as I was out the door.

I found Miss Lydia sipping iced tea in the kitchen and poured myself a glass. She slid a fat manila envelope across the table after I sat down.

I slipped the sheaf of papers out and read "Last Will and Testament" across the top of the first page. Tried to say, "Oh no, Miss Lydia—" but she cut me off.

"Oh, now, I don't plan to go anywhere anytime soon, so don't get your undies in a bunch."

It didn't work. I couldn't laugh and my hands were shaking.

She said, "Read. Read first and talk later."

So I read. There was a lot that might have been written in Portuguese for what I understood. It must make lawyers feel smarter to pretend they have their own language. But the gist of the thing was that everything went to me. The house, the land, the money, the car. Everything.

A maintenance allowance for the house would be mine no matter when she died. The rest would be held in a trust, if need be, until I turned eighteen.

My teeth were chattering when I finished. I looked up and told her, "It's not fair."

"For me to do what I want with my own money?" she asked.

"I don't deserve this," I started.

She was calm as can be. "Who does deserve it, then?"

She had me there. I fumbled the pages back into their envelope.

"Billie Marie." The way she pronounced it I knew she had rehearsed a speech. "I wanted you to know what was in it. This is a copy—the original is with Ernest Troutman in Milton. When I'm gone you can do whatever you want. I don't care if you give away every penny after your college has been paid for."

"But I'm not—" I began.

"Oh yes, you are," she finished. She was nodding. Agreeing with herself. "If I'm still alive, I'll kick your behind all the way there if I have to."

I had to smile at that image.

". . . and if I'm gone, well . . ." She went blank for a second. Then a wicked grin spread across her face. "I'll haunt you till you go, that's what I'll do."

College. She was going to send me to college. No matter what Daddy said. No matter what he thought, I was going to college. A pulse throbbed at my temple. Then I had another thought.

"What about Harlan?" I asked.

She answered with a shrug that said, "What *about* Harlan?"

I said, "I mean, shouldn't he—shouldn't you—" then caught myself. I had no business telling her what to do with her money. But maybe I did. No, I couldn't. My thoughts were fragments.

Miss Lydia was nodding. She had thought about this. "Harlan's parents likely expect him to go to school and would have the money to pay for it, too. Or if they don't— well, honey, scholarships are still a whole lot easier to come by for boys than girls. It's not fair, but—"

"But what if, what if—" The least possibility of going off and leaving Harlan down on the farm felt like a betrayal.

"If all else fails," she went on, "then either you or I can do what needs to be done when the time comes." She nodded at the envelope between us. "There's enough there for two college educations. More than enough."

A shudder shook my backbone. It was starting to sound like blood money.

"Honey." Miss Lydia reached and patted my hand. "Like I said, I have no plans to go anywhere. But the fact is, someday I will go. And I wanted to let you know about this now because you need to start planning for that. *And* for college. I had a notion your peckerhead daddy's words were still stuck in your head and your face is telling me I was right."

I was pretty sure the idea of college would grow on me. But life without her? Plan to give up life as I knew it now? I was still in a daze when I got home.

It was hours before it registered that she had called Daddy a peckerhead.

Chapter Twenty-Nine

It might have all been written on my forehead, self-conscious as I felt. Harlan asked once what was wrong. I told him I couldn't talk about it and he was so understanding I wanted to brain him. It seemed like the least he could do was hound me with questions until I broke down and told him without it being my fault.

My studying took on an urgency. Harlan and I had pushed so far beyond our class it was a laugh but now it wasn't nearly far enough for me. I went from book to book at such a frantic pace I wasn't learning anything. That made me panic even more.

Then one day during study hour Harlan told me to lighten up and that was all it took for me to come unglued. I started screaming with all the logic of a newborn baby, then collapsed in a heap and commenced to cry like one. He somehow got me up and on his lap. Sat there rocking while I soaked his shirt.

He petted my hair and said, "Shhh," in my ear. I

couldn't remember anyone but Miss Lydia ever giving me such comfort and that made me cry all the more.

But nobody can cry forever, even if they want to. After a while I became aware I was on Harlan's lap. My arms were around his neck. His were around my waist. I lifted my head from his shoulder, our cheeks brushed, and then we were kissing. I'm pretty sure I started it.

I felt that first kiss in every cell of my body. And then some.

If I'd ever thought about it I would have predicted any speck of romance at all would start our friendship down the road to ruin. But when it happened it was like Harlan and I had both been holding our breath without realizing it. Now we could let go and breathe. It felt that natural.

I asked him to leave his truck at school that day and walk with me to Miss Lydia's. On the way I told him about her will.

He wasn't a bit surprised. "Well, good God, Billie Marie," is what he said. "You're all the family she's got. What would you expect?"

And I loved that thought so very much it began to feel all right.

I found my way onto Harlan's lap again during study hour the next day and after a little nuzzling said, "Should we tell them?"

He frowned. "Tell who, what?"

"Our parents? Miss Lydia? About us?"

He gave me a little kiss on the neck that made my pulse flutter and said, "Billie Marie, if Miss Lydia didn't know before we did I'll eat my hat. And just what would you tell your parents?"

"Um . . . that we're boyfriend and girlfriend now?" Those words sounded so stupid out loud I cringed.

He said, "And . . . how is that different than before?"

"Well, completely," I told him.

"For me too," he smiled, "but how would you describe what's different to them?"

I shrugged.

"You want to tell them . . . we've started . . . making out? Scare them into watching us? Maybe even trying to keep us apart? Teenage hormones and all that?"

I jumped up like his lap had caught fire. "No." I smoothed my skirt and sat down in my own chair. The heat spread to my cheeks and my eyes started to sting. I hadn't thought about kissing Harlan as leading anywhere.

But maybe he had. He would, wouldn't he? That's how boys were. Teenage hormones and all that.

"What? What happened? What's the matter?" Harlan's eyes were huge. I shook my head. I couldn't say anything.

Never mind that I knew Harlan so completely we were practically extensions of the same person. Suddenly he was a stranger, that *Y* chromosome of his jumping out like a roadblock between us. My breathing turned ragged and I wanted to bolt.

He leaned forward, took both my hands in his and started rubbing his thumbs over my knuckles. I tried to pull away. I didn't want to be touched, not even by him. Ever again. I got my hands free and crossed them under my arms in a self-hug.

Harlan studied me a good while before saying, "Billie Marie, I don't know what you're afraid of, but I would hope you know I'd sooner throw myself into the river than hurt you. Ever. You have to trust me on that."

I turned away because he was looking me in the eye. How could I explain that "trust" had turned out to be the biggest word I knew? The one with the sharpest edges, for sure. I didn't answer him.

He was hurt. Of course. He was quiet the rest of the day and drove off after school without saying good-bye. I felt it as a physical ache in my chest. There's a reason they came up with the image of a little guy shooting arrows as a symbol for falling in love.

I knew I couldn't bring myself near what I'd have to tell Harlan to make him understand. I spent a long while in my room that night searching the mirror for answers, but that girl didn't have any either. That was okay. I didn't trust her either.

The next day Harlan and I had not said so much as

hello by time for study hour. I walked onto the stage with a huge volume from the encyclopedia, figuring I could hide behind it for an hour even if my stomachache wouldn't let me concentrate. Then I heard his voice behind me say, "Stop right there. And don't turn around."

I froze. I was a rabbit and he'd whistled.

He cleared his throat and told my back, "I'm not sure what happened here yesterday, but I know when I said you had to trust me you looked like I'd knocked the wind out of you with a baseball bat. So I'm just going to ask if you can at least give me benefit of the doubt. Have a little faith. That's all."

Trust. Faith. I couldn't speak above a whisper. "What's the difference?"

"Well, let's see," he said. "I know for a fact you have faith in God, Billie Marie, but that doesn't mean you would step out in front of a train because you trust him to save you, does it?"

Not a solitary smart aleck thought came into my head. That's how rootless I felt.

"You be just as careful as you need to be, Billie Marie. But you know me. Remember that."

My ears burned and my mind's eye showed me Harlan at age eleven scowling while he asked me to play baseball. Then I turned and saw the face he'd grown into at sixteen. It looked worried but resolute. I was the only other person in the world.

I walked over, wrapped my arms around his neck and laid my head in the hollow of his shoulder. He took a deep breath and rested his hands at the small of my back. It wasn't a hug, but more like dancing without moving our feet.

Come to find out, time doesn't make exceptions when good things fall from the sky any more than it does when a tragedy smacks you upside the head. So after that little bump our lives just kept going on. Miss Lydia tried to hide her smile whenever she saw us touch hands or look at each other so moony we forgot what we were saying.

Harlan had been right—there really was no reason to tell anyone anything. We'd gone to a movie together once in a while ever since he got his license. It seemed silly to announce that we held hands during the show, and now we kissed good night when Harlan dropped me off. For everything to be so completely different, it was strange how very little had changed.

For so long my heart had felt like it was closed into a fist around the secrets Miss Lydia and I shared. Now it opened up to make room for all it needed to hold. That was the biggest difference to me.

A few days after Miss Lydia bought the Caddie, Mama

noticed that the grout between the tiles in our bathroom looked dingy and she decided I should clean it. Thoroughly and painstakingly. With an old toothbrush, baking soda, and peroxide. I almost busted out laughing when she told me—it was like something out of a reform school movie on the late, late show.

Each night for a week she came in to call me for dinner and blew on about what a good job I was doing and what a wonderful difference it was going to make. She was using the same chore both to punish me and to try flattering her way into my good graces. A few years earlier it would have driven me nuts.

I decided to borrow a page from Miss Lydia's book instead.

The first day there was no more grout to clean I went home earlier than usual and baked a carrot cake. I didn't much care for the stuff, but of course I knew it was Mama's favorite. I even made the cream cheese frosting that always puckered my lips. We had some used birthday candles in the silverware drawer—I have no idea why she had saved them. I put one on the cake and lit it when I heard the car in the driveway.

Mama walked in with a sack from Smith Hardware and eyed that cake like its candle was a lit fuse. "What's this?" she said.

I hadn't planned it out in detail, so I said the first thing that came into my head: "Happy birthday!"

She looked peeved. "My birthday's in September, Billie. Surely you know that."

"Well, then, SURPRISE!" I yelled. I gave her my best beauty pageant smile.

Mama's jaw dropped and I waited. She started chuckling. I exhaled and laughed along with her.

Finally she wiped at her eyes and said, "Well, should I make a wish?"

I said, "Sure!" and she closed her eyes for a couple of seconds before she whooshed out the candle. Then she looked up at me with an expression I'd never seen.

It was a look that started me wondering. If her gratitude was genuine, did my intentions really matter?

Her purse was still hanging on her arm and she handed me a dollar out of her billfold. "No use having cake without ice cream," she said. "Run up to the elevator and get a half gallon."

When I walked back in a few minutes later she had saucers out and was cutting the cake. "What the—?" I mentally backed up and started over. "I mean, I thought we'd wait for Daddy."

Her mouth barely turned up at one corner when she looked up and said, "Why? It's not *his* birthday." We both giggled and I said a great big "thank you" to Miss Lydia in my head.

I set the ice cream on the table and went for a big spoon. "Shouldn't we wait till after supper at least?" I don't know why I felt like I had to be the grown-up.

Mama straightened up, hands on hips, and surveyed the table. "Vegetable, dairy . . . you put eggs in the cake?"

I nodded.

"Protein," she went on. "I think any home ec teacher would say we're covered." We giggled some more.

We had demolished half the cake and most of the ice cream when Daddy walked in later, and I suppose we looked like a couple of raccoons caught in the trash barrel. "What are you celebrating?" he asked.

A couple of seconds went by and I said, "Mama's birthday," and she and I both burst out laughing.

He frowned, looked over at the empty stovetop, then turned and started pulling sandwich stuff out of the refrigerator. I looked at Mama and she shrugged.

I had never found her on the same side as me across from Daddy. On anything. That was one momentous sandwich he made.

The carrot cake, even if my motive for making it had not been pure, was enough to buy me a good long honeymoon period with Miss Lydia and her Cadillac.

When we went to town on errands, it was like the old days, just the two of us laughing, telling stories, and singing songs. I had her all to myself and didn't feel guilty one bit. She was my true family. And I was all the family she had.

The day before Easter we hit the Milton Library and the grocery store and lightened the dime store by three big Easter baskets before we headed for home. Miss Lydia and I were swapping Easter Bunny stories and I had my eyes on the road. All at once a terrible moan came out of her.

I hit the brakes and swerved onto the shoulder. When I could look, the hair stood up on my neck. The right side of her face looked like it was melting. She was slumped against the door.

I squealed through a U-turn and then floored it. We were doing ninety when we passed the city limits sign, and I barely slowed down for that. Just laid on the horn every time we blew through a stop sign and thought *God help the person who hits this tank.*

I pulled right up into the ambulance bay at the back of the hospital and left my door swinging open. A nurse was walking into the emergency room. I spun her around and yanked her out to the Caddie, no time to waste on words.

They were fast, I'll tell you that. A TV doctor would be pressed to beat their time. They had Miss Lydia on a gurney and inside the emergency room before I could draw breath to tell her everything would be okay.

A security guard showed up and told me I had to

move the Cadillac to the parking lot. I argued with him and tried to give him the key, but there was nothing doing but I run and do it myself. I felt like I was letting Miss Lydia down, giving something worse a chance to happen by leaving even for a minute.

There are three hard chairs outside that windowless room and that's where I spent the next two hours. It felt like eight, it felt like a lifetime, sitting there alone. I wanted to call Harlan so badly but didn't know how far it was to the closest pay phone and couldn't make myself leave again. I tried to think about him so hard that he'd just *know* he should come.

I prayed, but not to God. To Miss Lydia. "Don't leave me. Please don't. I know you have to go sometime, but please, not yet. I'll try to get ready, honest I will. But not now. Not yet. Please. . . ."

She stayed.

I jumped up when the gurney pushed the doors open. Dr. Strunk and his big belly blocked me and I couldn't get close enough to see. He motioned me aside. The rest of the crew moved down the hall without a sound. Pallbearers for the living.

"Billie, isn't it?"

He'd only seen me a billion times in my life. I nodded.

"Good work, getting her here so quickly. You probably saved her life."

I almost fainted.

He went on, "It was a stroke. A fairly mild one, I believe, but at her age we won't know what the ... extent will be for a couple of days. She'll live, but she's got a rough road just ahead."

I gulped. "Can I see her?"

He took off his glasses and rubbed his eyes. "I don't think that's a good idea right now," he said. "She's ... pretty-well sedated and probably wouldn't know you were there anyway."

"I just want to tell her I love her." I was prepared to grab the sleeves of his white coat and beg.

He stared at the floor and sighed. "Well, I suppose we could all stand to hear that."

I was already five steps gone when he called, "Don't stay long."

She looked so small in that bed. Her breathing was raspy and even so it was the finest sound I'd ever heard. Her eyes were closed and half her face drooped like it had witnessed something sorrowful the other half hadn't seen.

I made the sign of the cross. It just seemed appropriate. "I love you, Miss Lydia," I whispered.

I thought she was sleeping but her left eyelid fluttered. Her mouth worked a bit. It cost so much effort I put a finger to her lips.

Her left hand inched upward. After a minute that felt

like agony to me, she rested it on her breast with her finger pointing to her heart. I gave her a light kiss. Mumbled
something about seeing her soon. Hauled butt out of
there before I started crying.

That night Mama told me since I had never driven
alone, I wasn't to drive in to the hospital after school. But
it was planting season and she wasn't getting home before
dark any night of the week. The Caddie made the trip so
many times I could have let loose the steering wheel and
given it its head like a barn-bound horse. Harlan went
with me whenever he could.

Miss Lydia being a stubborn old cuss paid off in
spades during her rehabilitation. Within a week you
could understand half of what she said. Within another
she was shuffling along behind a walker. Nurses said
they'd seen people twenty years younger never make it
that far.

The doctor wanted to send her to a nursing home
when she was well enough. But every time he raised the
subject, she fixed him with her one good eye and said,
"Hooome." It sounded half hymn and half dirge. Nobody
could pretend they didn't understand.

Miss Lydia had been in the hospital nearly two
months by the time school let out in May. The first day I
stayed home I cooked a huge dinner and Harlan brought
his parents to our house around the time my folks were

coming in. Mama and Daddy were surprised, of course, but I had counted on the fact that they wouldn't yell at me in front of other people. Our table had been used so little in recent years it felt really strange to sit there in a group of six.

Harlan and I took turns talking and laid out our case for bringing Miss Lydia home. When we started out it looked like we were going to have a snowball's chance in July. We were looking at a Mount Rushmore of parents. But we stayed calm and took it point by point. Just like we had practiced. We were both pretty good debaters by then.

Finally it seemed like they had run out of questions. Everybody sat there waiting. Then Mama spoke up and said, "Well, I can't argue with her wanting to come home. I imagine we'll all want to when the time comes. And it's not like she has anybody else. As far as I'm concerned, you can try."

That made everybody sit up. The other grown-ups looked at her like she was crazy.

Her chin jutted out and a faint pink spot appeared on each of her cheeks. "When's the last time any of you started out on a project with a guarantee it was going to work out just the way you wanted it to?" she asked them.

Nobody answered.

"That's all anybody ever really does, is try."

She looked around the table and I watched the other parents each cow a little in turn. Mama has looks that can burn better than a magnifying glass in the sunshine.

She turned to me and her expression still contained a challenge. I didn't get it at first. But something in her face and something about sitting there at that table started conjuring up a carrot cake, ice cream, and Daddy making his own dinner while she and I sat on the other side of an unseen fence.

And I got it. Ever since I'd confronted her about the son she had wanted instead of me, she'd tried to make up. Clumsy gestures offered from time to time. I hadn't bought into any of them and she knew it.

So here was the granddaddy of all offerings. Taking a stand for me against all of the others. It was an act of penitence.

If I had still needed her to be my mother I might have forgiven her everything on the spot.

Mrs. Willits finally allowed, "I don't suppose the decision would be irreversible. If it didn't work out . . ." She looked to the men, but they had both just realized they were overdue for fingernail inspection.

We had a meeting at the hospital the next day. Dr. Strunk, the charge nurse from rehab, Harlan and his parents, Mama, Daddy, me. Dr. Strunk must have been building up quite an aggravation with Miss Lydia, to come off the golf course on a Sunday and settle the matter.

Harlan and I made our pitch and our parents backed us up. The others had all decided overnight that they agreed with Mama—or at least none of them were ready to take her on. They explained all we had already done for Miss Lydia. Almost five years' worth. And Dr. Strunk listened to them. God and parents know a doctor isn't going to take the word of a couple of teenagers.

When Doc finally gave his okay it was more like he was washing his hands in Pontius Pilate's basin. Harlan and I didn't care. We were giving Miss Lydia what she wanted. We were bringing her home.

Chapter Thirty

When our folks went back to chores that day, Harlan and I went to Miss Lydia's. He had built handrails by the steps a year before. Now we found enough lumber in her garage to build a ramp out front. I pried open six rusty cans and found the red door paint. When we were finished, it looked like we had rolled out the red carpet.

Then we moved inside. All the big dining room furniture went out to the kitchen. Miss Lydia's bedroom came downstairs. It made sense to store the dining room stuff up in her room, but I couldn't make that sit right in my head.

I explained, "That's like telling her she'll never move back up there. That we're calling this permanent."

I swear Harlan's eyes get even bluer when they're sad.

"I know, I know," I said. "But one step at a time, okay?"

Of course it wasn't really about Miss Lydia. We could say the dining room set was on the roof or that we had sold it to gypsies and she would have to take our word for it.

"Okay. Where, then?" Harlan isn't nearly as stubborn as me, so he'd learned to pick his battles.

I couldn't bear to junk up my favorite bedroom. "The . . . closed room," I decided. Harlan just nodded and picked up a chair.

There was an overlay of pine cleaner and air spray in Curtis's room, but it was like perfume on a pig. His smell still hung so thick in the air I wanted to wipe it off my skin. It made my lungs feel spongy, breathing it in.

I ran up and down the stairs partly so my huffing could be laid to exertion, but I also wanted to slam that door as soon as possible.

We were both sweaty after we wrestled the table and buffet up there. We sat down in the kitchen with a pitcher of iced tea Miss Lydia had made one Saturday morning two months earlier. She had expected to drink it that afternoon.

I started a shopping list. We discussed handgrips by the toilet and the fact that Miss Lydia must have seen this day coming when she had a shower put in her downstairs bathroom years before.

Harlan was talking about the problem of fastening hardware to tile when I said, "It was him." I hadn't even known it was coming out. But there it was, plain as if I'd set it on a platter between us.

"Huh?" Harlan frowned, his mind still at the hardware store.

All I could do for an answer was turn red. Our eyes locked and I watched his face go from preoccupied to bewildered. Then it tensed, one muscle at a time, into something fearsome.

"It *was* him." His voice sounded so hard. It had quit breaking months before, but I hadn't noticed how deep it had become.

I couldn't trust my own voice so I nodded. My ears felt like they were on fire and I clenched my jaw to stop my teeth from rattling.

I had a fleeting notion that Harlan was going to haul off and hit me—his eyes looked like they could spark a blaze. I counted the heaves of his chest. Eleven before he spoke.

"So Miss Lydia—"

"No! Don't say it!" I shouted. But I know my face told him "yes." We sat frozen for so long I nearly passed out from holding my breath.

Harlan's fist came down on the table so hard both glasses overturned. I let out a shriek and jumped up for a towel. Then he did something I'd never known him to do. He started crying.

"I'm sorry," I said. I wasn't sure he could hear me, but the words were more for me anyway. "I'm so sorry. I shouldn't have told you. Not now. Not like this."

When he stood his chair tipped and slid into the wall. I barely glimpsed the pure shipwreck of his face before he grabbed me. Bones crunched in my back as he squeezed. Then we were on the floor, me on his lap, his head on my shoulder. I don't know how much time passed before he found his voice.

"I—I'm so sorry," he rasped.

"So am I," I told him. I smoothed his perfect black hair. "But I'm okay now, and it—"

"No!" he yelled. "I—should have . . . I didn't protect you."

Well. That made absolutely no sense. But I had drunk from the well of unreason often enough to think I understood the taste in his mouth.

"It's okay, Harlan," I said. "You didn't know. You *couldn't* have known." We rocked back and forth, a solitary unit.

The words fought past something in his throat. "No," he said. "It's not okay."

"No, you're right, it's not," I agreed. I remembered how I had felt upstairs in Curtis's room earlier and shuddered. "But . . . he didn't get away with it, Harlan. Remember. He paid."

"Goddamn BASTARD!" He yelled so close to my right ear it started a dull ringing.

Then I understood. Curtis had been punished, but not by Harlan's hand. And Harlan loved us so much, Miss Lydia and me, of course he would own part of our pain. Curtis's account wouldn't be cleared until Harlan exacted some payment of his own. Even if it was only to wish damnation on a man no doubt already in hell.

Chapter Thirty-One

By the time we got Miss Lydia in and settled we were all exhausted and Harlan and I were exchanging looks. I wondered if this was what it was like to bring a new baby home and finally be left alone. Just the two of you and a bundle of endless need. It felt like stepping onto a carousel that wasn't going to stop and let us off anytime in the foreseeable future.

But it turned out like anything else. You establish a routine, that's what life becomes, and you do what needs to be done. And Miss Lydia, she fought to do what she could for herself.

Some mornings she was already dressed when I got there. Sometimes she needed help. I told her that first day I had seen naked girls before and she was no more impressive than the rest of them.

She could pack more into half a face than most people with all their features and she learned to fix her good eye on me in an "I'll get you" stare that cracked me up. She could barely lift one corner of her mouth to smile, but she could still laugh and we did plenty of that.

It was an effort for her to form words, so she made them count. Mostly she said "thank you."

I'd check on her in the morning—see that she'd eaten and made it to the bathroom, finish dressing her if necessary. I'd go back home and catch up with our house, then I'd bring home the mail and start cooking. I made so many trips across the street that after a few days I combined the pantries and did all the meals at her house. If I planned well enough, in a couple of hours' time I could have lunch and dinner taken care of for everybody.

"Everybody" was Miss Lydia and me at lunchtime, us two plus Harlan for dinner, and Mama and Daddy when I saw their truck pull in. Harlan's mother started sending a big casserole or pie every few days too. I rained blessings on her for that.

Harlan would do his morning chores at home and show up after lunch to save me some little effort in the kitchen. Then he'd stay until time for me to put Miss Lydia to bed. He did all the dishes and most of the laundry and gave me a break whenever I needed more time at home. He's a good team player.

Miss Lydia shuffled her walker between the bed, the bathroom, the kitchen, and her TV chair. It was a full-time job. A lot of people would have packed it in and stayed in bed. Not her.

Most of the time we understood her, but some words had just gotten out of her reach. She worked at it. Lord, did she work. One day she said something that sounded like, "cheese 'n die," over and over until we were both frustrated.

I finally ran across the street and came back with the Ouija board that had gathered dust under my bed for years. Laid it across her lap and put a pencil in her left hand.

She labored after those letters, pointing to them one by one. "G . . . E . . . S . . . U . . . N . . . D . . . H . . . E . . . I . . ." I announced. When she pointed to *T*, she dropped the pencil and wobbled her cup of tea into the air.

"Gesundheit?"

Her good eye twinkled.

"You've been trying to tell me 'GESUNDHEIT?'" We'd worked for so long I'd forgotten the sneeze that came before. I laughed so hard I cried.

About a week after we brought her home the refrigerator was empty and utility bills were piling up. I didn't know what to do and asked Harlan.

He said, "Ask Miss Lydia."

Well, sure.

She was nodding even before I finished the first

sentence. "Eel," she said, then shook her head. "Wool," she got out second try. She mock-spat to show her disgust.

"Hold on," I told her. I spent a few minutes trying those two words out to see what they felt like in my mouth. "Will?" I ventured.

"Ding!" she cried. She'd taken to using that in place of "yes." "Up," she told me, looking toward the stairs.

There was a two-drawer oak file cabinet in her bedroom. I asked if that was what she meant and got "dinged" again.

The instant I opened the top drawer, I saw. On top of the manila envelope containing her will was a whole book of signed checks. Fifty of them.

Pretty thorough planning. I had to wonder, though, what went through her mind the day she sat signing check after check, building a hedge against the day she might not be able to. Bravery has a lot more faces than I used to think.

Every couple of weeks she had a doctor's appointment and Harlan came along to help. We all slept well those nights, I'll tell you. Dr. Strunk, amazed as he continued to be, had to admit she was doing fine.

So went the days, the weeks, a month, and then two. I was plenty tired by bedtime every night but couldn't think of anything I would rather be doing with my summer. Once in a while my stomach tightened at the thought of school starting up again, but Miss Lydia was okay for a few hours on her own. I could always run home at lunchtime. We'd get by.

Tuesday morning I knew something was wrong the second I opened the back door. The air was charged. I felt that energy even before my nose picked up on bad news. I counted ten deep breaths before I went on in.

She was still in bed and the good side of her face was tight with fear. "It's okay," I heard myself say. I smoothed back her hair. "It'll be all right."

A tear formed in the corner of her eye.

"Can you talk, Miss Lydia?" I crooned. "Can you tell me what's going on?" I was panicking on the inside but resolute not to let it show. Facing someone you love who is terrified will let you do that.

She tried but no sound came out. Not that it was necessary—it was obvious what had happened. Another stroke had come for her in the night.

I laid a hand on her forehead. Willed myself not to shake. "Don't you worry, Miss Lydia. It'll be all right. I'll go call for help right now."

"AAAHHHW!" is what it sounded like she said, but her intent was clear. She was saying no.

"Oh. Well, okay, we'll have to see." My mind was racing too fast to form a meaningful thought. Slow down. One thing at a time. "First things first." I'm pretty sure I said that out loud. "Let's get you some fresh clothes."

I was glad she couldn't lift her head to be mortified by the mess she was lying in.

I went to the bathroom for a washcloth, towel, and basin of warm water. "May as well sponge off a little while we're at it," I said. Tried to keep my tone light.

How could I not call for an ambulance? I thought. A doctor at the very least? Then I told myself again to slow down. One thing at a time. And just then the most important thing was trying to preserve any remaining dignity this woman was holding onto.

I rolled her side to side, slipping the sheet underneath and replacing it with a thick towel. Folded the mess inside a bundle as I worked. Took it straight to the washer and dumped it in.

I scoured my mind for a song. One she loved. While I bathed her and pretended it was the most natural thing in the world, I sang. "Casey would waltz with the strawberry blonde and the band played on. . . ." I smiled up at her between lines.

I had never understood how mothers could change dirty diapers and keep their good humor, but now I did. When it's someone you love you do what needs to be done. Period.

If it's possible to show both sadness and gratitude in a face that close to immobile, she did.

I got her into a clean nightgown and rolled her side to side onto clean sheets. Tucked her in and asked if she wanted some tea. She blinked a few times and squinted her left eye. Trying to smile.

I chewed all ten nails down waiting for the teapot to whistle. I would call Harlan first chance. I couldn't see what else there was to do. I could ask if she was sure she didn't want to call for help, but I knew what that answer would be.

If she went to the hospital she'd never come home again. She knew that.

I sat on the edge of the bed and tipped teaspoons of warm, sweet tea into her mouth. Then I remembered I had laid out a chicken for today's lunch because she had been doing better with finger food than utensils. Time to rethink that. Besides, her dentures hadn't fit all that well after the first stroke. They were useless now.

It took half an hour to finish the cup. I kissed her cheek and told her to get some rest. She was snoring little kitten sounds before I got to the kitchen.

I sat and watched her sleep the rest of the morning. Prayed to every deity I had ever heard of to show me the way. None of them did.

I thought Harlan might be in his house at lunchtime. He was. I answered his hello with, "Oh, thank God."

He said, "What is it?"

I tried to back up and soften it. "We've got a bit of a problem here, Harlan."

"I know!" he snapped. "Quit dinking around and tell me what it is!" So much for tap dancing. Harlan is like a watchdog, always one snapping twig away from high alert.

"Miss Lydia's had another stroke," I told him.

"When?"

"Sometime in the night. I don't know exactly."

"Are you calling from the hospital?" he asked. If Harlan has ever lost his ability to track coherent thought I've not been a witness.

"Nooo," I said. I was one sentence away from feeling stupid.

He said, "The ambulance is on its way then." Yep, there it was.

"Uh, no. She didn't want me to—"

He pounced. "Billie Marie, are you *nuts*?" I heard him breathing. Trying to stand down. He switched to a tone you might use with a dog that may or may not be rabid.

"Sweetheart," he said. Blood rushed to my face. He had never called me that. "You've got to call for help. You just—"

"I can't!" I felt like stamping my foot. Like that would be effective. Especially over the phone. "This is Miss Lydia's house!" I went on. "It's her life! She's still *in* there,

Harlan!" and he knew I didn't mean in her former din-ing room.

One, two, three breaths. "Okay," he said, "I'm on my way."

She roused a little when we walked in together. Harlan had only seen her in bed at the hospital, but he jollied right up to her with his best bedside manner.

"Well, now," he said, taking her hand between both of his. "Billie Marie tells me you've had another adventure."

She puckered her lips in displeasure.

"I know, I know," he nodded. "Not the kind you ordered. Well, you know, I think the first order of busi-ness is to take inventory. Can you talk at all, Miss Lydia?"

Her mouth opened to emit an "aaauuuww." Mine dropped open too. Assessing the damage. It should have been the first thing I thought of.

"Uh-huh," Harlan encouraged. "Anything else?" But her next attempt sounded much the same.

"Okay." He seemed to have a mental checklist. "Obviously you can blink. You can swallow?" he asked. We watched her Adam's apple bob.

"Can you turn your head for me, Miss Lydia?" You could read the determination in her eyes, but she just couldn't do it.

"Okay!" Harlan said, as though this was progress.

"How about your arm, Miss Lydia? Can you lift it?"

We stared at her left arm with the concentration of a couple at a séance trying to levitate a table. After much too long, her fingers started flexing. Out and back. She couldn't quite make a fist.

Harlan said, "All right! Some fine motor movement, not so much on the large muscle groups." I looked at him in wonder.

He loosened the sheet at the foot of the bed. "This little piggy?" he said, pinching her big toe.

Her left eye squinted. Her new smile. She could wiggle her toes, but her foot and leg stayed put.

Harlan pulled up a chair and smiled at her. Then he said, "Well, Miss Lydia, I know the hospital's not your favorite hotel but I really think we ought to let Doc Strunk know what's going on."

"AAAAAW!" she said. Tears started down her left cheek.

Harlan looked stricken. I gave him a look that said "I told you so," but there was no satisfaction in it.

I stood and smoothed Miss Lydia's hair like before. "It's okay," I cooed. "It's gonna be all right." I caught Harlan's eye, then told her, "You rest now, okay? We've got you all worn out."

We retired to the kitchen and flung furious whispers across the table. "I can't do it," I told him. "Maybe you can, but I won't have it on my conscience."

"Don't make me the bad guy!" Harlan hissed.

Deep breaths. One, two, three. "There is no bad guy," I said. "There's just an old woman who . . . who wants to die at home."

My eyes welled up and Harlan's mirrored them. It was intimate as a hug.

"Sweetheart," he said. My tears overflowed. "Your parents are going to call town when they find out, you know that."

I said, "I won't tell them!"

"Sweetheart." It wasn't so affectionate this time. "She can't be left alone anymore. Think about it. *You can't go home.* Don't you think they'll notice?"

But I hadn't thought ahead at all. If I had, I would have realized I was already beaten. It wasn't fair. I shouldn't be in this position, let alone feel like a failure.

This was Miss Lydia. She deserved so much better.

My chin came up and I wiped my face. "Well, then, I've at least got until dark," I told him. "I need you to go to town for some supplies—maybe there's some way to get this under control. . . ." I was already reaching for a notebook and pen.

Harlan took the list when I finished. "Bedpan?" he asked. His eyebrows shot up.

"It's better than diapers, don't you think?" I hadn't

meant to sound angry and tried to soften it a notch. "Medical supply store, Folger and Aldrich."

He went on. "Drinking straws, the kind that bend. Baby food." He stared like the words made no sense. Looked up. "What kind of baby food?"

I felt my confidence wilt. "An assortment, I guess. I don't know."

He wrapped his arms around me and laid his cheek next to mine. "Hang on, Billie Marie. Hang on. Right now we're just talking about the rest of the day and you already know you can do that."

I can do this. I can do this. It became my mantra after he left.

Miss Lydia had wet herself while we talked in the kitchen. This time I changed her and the bed to the tune of "Take Me Out to the Ballgame." The tension in her face lessened a little. But not as much as I'd hoped.

Her television was on a rolling cart in the living room. I moved it so she could see it and turned it on, then set her glasses on her face and went to the kitchen. A few minutes later I came back with a tray. Said, "Hey, you know what? I forgot to make you breakfast! So here you go, oatmeal for lunch." I pretended to be engrossed in her soap opera while I spoon-fed her.

I can do this. I can do this.

We got through the afternoon. After some trial and

error, we settled on "ee" as a signal for the bedpan, and Harlan made up work to do in another room often enough she never had to say it in front of him.

By the time shadows started stretching dark fingers across the room we had found something of a rhythm and I dreaded the conversation with my folks that was coming. When their headlights panned the room and turned into the driveway across the street, Harlan and I inhaled in unison.

I can do this. "Time to take my folks dinner, Miss Lydia," I lilted. "I'll be back in a bit." But her face was full of fear and Harlan gave me a grim little smile.

Before Mama could head for the living room with her plate, I said, "I need to talk to you two," and they both froze. It would have been funny under other circumstances. I folded my hands on the table. In slow motion, they took their old spots.

I told them how I had found Miss Lydia that morning, minus the laundry problem. Described the rest of the day as a recitation of fact. Finished with no question, no demand, no call to action. Just waited.

Daddy spoke first with, "You can't do this." He didn't say, ". . . and you know that," but it was in his voice.

I said, "That's exactly what Harlan said until he told her we had to call for help and heard her answer." I looked them in the eye, one after another. "I can't do it.

He can't do it. If you're gonna do it, you'll have to go over there and tell her yourself."

They held one of those eyes-only consultations married couples do. Then Mama spoke. "Billie," she said. "You've already done far more than you were called on to do. And this is too much for anybody. Why on earth would you even try?"

"Because it's the right thing to do." How could a parent argue with that? I gave each in turn a steady gaze that dared them.

They partnered in another long look. Daddy reminded me, "School starts in less than two weeks." Logic always trumps emotion in his hand.

I said, "Maybe I'll have to give up when school starts. Maybe I'll have to give up tomorrow." I picked up speed. "But this is really important to her and I'm not sure I could ever forgive myself if I didn't try. So, please let me. Please."

No sound but my ragged breathing. Ten seconds. Twenty.

"It's against my better judgment . . ." Daddy started, and I jumped to my feet. Mama stood up too. For a second I was afraid she was going to block the door. I searched her face, but all I saw was a tired middle-aged woman waving a white flag.

I said, "Thanks, Mama," patted her shoulder and left. That was the most I could move toward a truce just then.

I splashed my face with cold water before going into Miss Lydia's room. Harlan's face was one big question mark.

"Okay, then!" I rubbed my hands together. "Who needs what?"

Seconds ticked by. Miss Lydia's lips puckered into the shape of a kiss.

Harlan contemplated his shoes a good while and then said, "Have you eaten today, Billie Marie?"

I guess I looked blank.

He said, "I didn't think so. Go eat something. Now."

Chapter Thirty-Two

Wednesday wasn't so bad. Harlan had made a pallet of quilts on the floor next to Miss Lydia and she slept through until about seven that morning. We passed a couple of hours with breakfast and morning ablutions.

She seemed at peace. I was so very thankful my folks had given me this chance.

Harlan showed up at noon with a big casserole dish and an accusing eye. "You haven't eaten, have you?" he said.

I hadn't.

After, I said I'd like to feed Miss Lydia lunch and go home for a shower and clean clothes. He assured me he could feed her if I told him what.

I sorted through the baby food he had brought from Milton and picked out some orange stuff and some green stuff. It all looked horrible.

"How do I heat it up?" he asked.

I have no idea where it came from but I said, "Boil

some water on the stove and set the jars in that for a while."

He looked at me like I had invented money.

I had my hand on the door before I thought. "Hey, and put it in little bowls, okay? She doesn't need to see the jars."

He blew me a kiss. I pretended to snatch it out of the air with my hand. It was the first time either of us had laughed since Monday.

I sent him to Milton that afternoon for a blender. I knew I could make food that tasted better than what was in those jars.

He came back with a bonus: a doorbell. He said, "You don't really want to sleep on the floor from now on, do you?"

Of course I didn't. I was already longing for the pink room upstairs.

"Okay, then," he said. He spliced the wire connected to the push button into an extension cord and used adhesive tape to fasten it to Miss Lydia's left index finger. Then he wired the bell part the same way and took it upstairs.

Miss Lydia had to focus herself and practice, but she could push the button with her thumb most tries. She crinkled her eye at Harlan. I gave him a big hug.

His mother called when she got home from work. He

assured her we were doing fine. My mother called when she got home too.

I started apologizing out of habit. "Oh, Mama, I forgot dinner," I said. "Miss Willits sent a big casserole with Harlan today, and I just didn't think to—"

"Billie. Stop it," she said.

I answered, "Yes, ma'am."

I heard her sigh. "I wanted to make sure everything's okay over there. I'd come over, but I don't know if Lydia wants—"

"That's okay," I broke in. "I'm pretty sure she doesn't. But yeah, we're doing just fine." I told her about the blender and the doorbell.

"All right," she said. "But call if you need anything."

"Okay," I told her. Before she could hang up I took a deep breath and said, "Mama?"

"What?"

"Thank you. I mean that."

"Uh-huh," she said. Her tone said she didn't trust me either.

The nightmare began almost as soon as Harlan left Wednesday night. I had given Miss Lydia her medicine, put her on the bedpan, tucked her in and told her good night. Upstairs, before I could even get into my night-gown, *Ding-dong.*

By Thursday morning I was ready to pitch that

damned bell out the second-story window.

I don't think I got more than twenty minutes sleep at a stretch and got up feeling worse than if it had been none at all. A lot was frustration. Miss Lydia couldn't tell me what she needed and, once we got past food, drink, and bedpan, I had limited inspiration to guess.

I tried changing her position. I tried fewer bedclothes. Then more. I tried aspirin ground up and mixed with water in a spoon. I tried prayer.

A couple of times I went running down the steps to find her sound asleep, thumb on the button.

I could tell she was as frustrated as I was and I'm pretty sure we both had a cry around five a.m. But it's all a blur and I might have dreamed that part.

Harlan got there by eleven with another bread pan full of his mother's cooking. He looked startled when he saw me. I hadn't looked in the mirror and didn't much care.

He sat me down and made me eat food I couldn't taste and then told me to go home for a shower and a nap. I knew I needed a shower, but told him I'd come back and take a nap in the pink room upstairs.

"Damnit, Billie Marie," he said, "sleep in your own bed for a couple of hours, would you?"

"Bedpan," I reminded him. He couldn't argue with that.

I didn't dry my hair or go for the mail. I was crawling under the pink comforter in fresh clothes twenty minutes later. About the time I closed my eyes the bell ding-donged.

I will never, ever have that kind of doorbell in any home I live in the rest of my life.

It was a bedpan call. After I'd emptied it and washed my hands I headed back up. I was having trouble separating desperation from exhaustion just then and didn't want to face Harlan again until I had rested.

I slept until the bell woke me up at four. I was a little hazy around the edges, but felt so much better I managed a smile.

But Harlan looked grim and Miss Lydia wouldn't meet my eye. Something in the air had changed while I slept and I got a sense of foreboding.

Harlan went to the kitchen and I sang "Don't Fence Me In" during bedpan duty. It didn't lighten the gloom any at all.

His mom called at five-thirty. Later I saw my parents' headlights swing by. When the phone rang again I motioned for Harlan to answer it. I wasn't sure I could inspire confidence in my abilities at that moment.

He hung up and pointed to a kitchen chair. I sat.

"What?" I said.

"We have to talk."

I snorted. "Yeah, I figured as much. Start." I didn't intend to be short, but wasn't sure I could rein it in either.

He fixed me with a big blue stare. "You've got to let her go, Billie Marie," he pronounced.

I waved my hands like I was erasing his words. "You know as well as I do she doesn't *want* to go, she wants to stay here—"

"That's not what I mean." It was the voice people use when they have a conversation inside a church. It was a voice you don't argue with. It scared me.

"I don't know what you mean—" I started.

But then I did.

"Oh, Harlan . . . oh." My scalp tingled. "I know I haven't done a very good job, but it's only been three days and I'll get better."

He looked so calm I wanted to shake him. He said, "You've done a perfect job. You've done everything anybody could do. More. And how many days does it feel like it's been?"

I tried to laugh. "Well, it *feels* like it's been about three months, but—" My voice sounded flat. Even to me.

"How long do you think it's felt like to Miss Lydia, lying there unable to move?" he asked.

I thought about her not meeting my eye and couldn't answer him.

"I know you want to do right by her." It was clear this was the next line of a speech he had written while I slept.

I lashed out in all directions at once. "How can you—how could I possibly—how *dare* you try to tell me—"

His eyes hadn't left my face. "I know you both pretty well, you know." He looked so sad. "And I love you both more than almost anything in the world."

I had daydreamed a whole list of scenarios built around the first time Harlan would tell me he loved me. None of them had looked anything like this.

"Do you really think she wants to live this way?" he asked.

I hadn't considered it. Shame on me.

"She's alive, sweetheart, but that's all you can say. She's got no life," he said. "And besides that, she knows school starts in a little over a week. You think she wants to put you through all this and still end up going to the hospital?"

Thinking one day at a time had not prepared me for this. I was shaking. "What . . . what are you saying I should do?" It was the voice of a little girl and it sounded like it was coming from elsewhere in the room.

One breath. Two. He said, "I don't think she'll go as long as she thinks you need her, Billie Marie."

She thought *I* needed *her*? I was the one answering the doorbell, emptying the bedpan, changing the sheets. . . .

But of course she did. Of course she did. Of course.

I was too empty to cry. "I don't know if I can do it, Harlan. I'm not that strong. I just . . . can't."

We sat there in silence. Hanging over our heads was the knowledge of what Miss Lydia had done for me. What she had found the strength to do. Somehow.

I was a coward and I knew it.

The night passed a little better than the one before, mainly because Miss Lydia made a mighty effort not to buzz as often. And it cost her. I found her soaked when I woke up in the morning and went down to check on her.

There was no longer a thing she could do for herself and she still didn't want to be a burden.

Her good eye didn't crinkle at my songs or jokes and my heart gained a little heft each time it didn't. Every minute she wouldn't look at me felt like an hour. The day crawled on.

Harlan came at the usual time and we went through the motions of our chores like a couple of robots. I don't think we exchanged five words before he left at bedtime. Miss Lydia wouldn't look at him, either.

This morning I took a long time with her bath. I washed her hair and curled it. I brushed it after it was dry and brushed it some more. She always liked that. I searched through her dresser to find her nicest nightgown

and some perfume that probably dated back to one
Christmas with Mr. Jenkins.

I didn't want to stop touching her.

I made creamed chicken and carrot puree for her
lunch and then smacked Harlan's hand away and fed her
myself before I went home. I ran the shower as hot as it
would get, then stood in the steam and scalded myself
raw.

I cursed and prayed, sometimes in the same breath. All
at the top of my lungs. There was nobody to hear.

I washed away the last four days.

When my hair was dry I twisted it up into a knot,
then dabbed on the first makeup I had worn all summer.
I dug through my closet and found a sundress Mama
always made me cover with a sweater for church. The
dress went over my head and I kicked the cardigan into a
corner.

I painted my fingernails bright red, then polished my
toenails to match. War paint. I slid on some strappy san-
dals with a small heel.

I can do this.

I hadn't bothered with jewelry all summer either, but
today I pinned the ruby heart to my bodice. Fastened the
ruby heart posts in my ears. Armor.

I can do this.

Harlan was surprised when he saw me. Then a look

of recognition came into his eyes and I gave him a look as sharp as a slap across the face. This was a mission now. It wouldn't advance the cause to turn all mealy inside.

I said, "I had an idea. How about going through some photo albums, Miss Lydia?" It had been over twenty-four hours since she'd met my eye and there was still no response.

"Harlan?" I said. "I got them out this morning. They're on Miss Lydia's bed upstairs." He jumped like I had goosed him with a cattle prod.

When he heard me finish "Jeannie With the Light Brown Hair" he knew the coast was clear. He came back with an armload of musty leather.

I picked one. "Let's start at the beginning, okay? This is Joe, and this is Charlie, and this is Robert. . . ." I had heard the story of each photo at least three times. I recited them as closely as I could to exactly as she had told them.

Harlan joined in. "This was the summer the boys took turns jumping off the shed and little Joe broke his arm," he said. I nodded him my approval and he looked relieved.

We knew them all and we told her own stories to her until our voices croaked. A few times she closed her eyes. After a few seconds we would pause. But each time she opened her eyes, whispering, "Ess," and we went on.

It was the best I knew to do, giving her life back to her one more time.

By the time we finished she needed to rest. While she slept I cooked a huge dinner and took most of it across the street. I stashed it in the refrigerator, took out a legal pad, and left a note on the table.

> *Mama and Daddy,*
> *Dinner's in the fridge ready to be heated up.*
> *We're having a real good day, so I had plenty*
> *of time to cook.*
> *Miss Lydia seems to need more sleep today,*
> *though, so please don't call tonight. You might*
> *wake her up.*
> *I'll call you if I need anything.*
>
> *Thanks,*
> *B.*

It was a long walk back across that street.

I fed Miss Lydia pureed roast beef, mashed potatoes, and gravy for dinner and she ate better than she had since the second stroke. I blessed each bite she managed.

Then she napped again. Harlan and I sat across the kitchen table from one another and rearranged the food on our plates in silence, like a couple whose marriage has outlived their interest in one another.

When I stacked the dishes I saw pink fingers reaching across the sky out the window above the sink. I checked to make sure Miss Lydia was still sleeping and slipped out the back door.

I didn't know Harlan had followed me until I felt his arm around my waist. I patted his hand and squeezed it. That was all the conversation we could muster.

When the last slice of orange disappeared over the horizon, I turned and hugged him. "You go on," I said.

It was clear he didn't want to. Before he could say anything I gave him a quick, hard kiss.

"Please, Harlan. Go home," I said. "We'll manage just fine."

He looked doubtful. But he ambled away, head hung low.

I held Miss Lydia's hand until she woke up and then I whispered her name to bring her all the way back to the room. She looked at me with no emotion I could detect.

I sang her favorite hymn, "In the Garden," during bedpan, but my voice fell flat and she was avoiding my eyes again.

After my hands were washed I stared into the bathroom mirror. Just until my face started to change. I told her, "You can do this."

I sat beside the bed and took Miss Lydia's hand again. I said her name. She stared at the opposite wall.

"Miss Lydia, I need you to look at me. I have something important to tell you."

Her eyes moved until they met mine, but they held no questions.

I leaned closer. "Miss Lydia," I said. "I want you to know that I understand now about loving someone. I can see it, loving somebody all the way from *A* to *Z*."

I waited. A look of cloudy confusion was my answer.

"I want to, with Harlan. I love him that much."

The clouds showed no sign of clearing.

"You know," I said, "a man and a woman. Together. I want to, with Harlan."

Her brow creased. Then her good eye registered a look of raw terror. God help me, I almost chuckled.

"No, no, no, now. Don't be scared for me," I told her. "I didn't say we were *going* to. Not any time soon for sure, maybe never. I don't know."

A silent question in response.

"I have lots of things to do first. I know that. Finish high school, maybe travel some. And Miss Lydia, did you know I'm going to college?" I summoned all the sunshine I could and beamed it into a smile.

Her face relaxed. I squeezed her hand.

"But I want to, Miss Lydia," I told her. "I understand

wanting to now. And isn't that what really matters?"

Ever so slowly, the left corner of her mouth rose a fraction.

"I'm okay. You don't have to worry about me anymore."

I can do this. I can do this.

"I know you're tired," I told her. "You're so tired. Get some good rest now. You've earned it."

Her hand started twitching. I let go. She bent her index finger upward. I frowned my stupidity.

With a mighty effort she said, "Arr."

Ar. I rolled this around in my mouth and finally thought I understood. "Heart?" I asked her.

She blinked several times. "Ess," she said.

I took her hand and laid it on her breast. Straightened her finger. Rested it at her heart.

"I love you, too, Miss Lydia. So very, very much." I kissed her cheek.

Her left eye crinkled.

"Now it's time to rest," I reminded her. "Good night."

It always takes me by surprise when I catch up to my thoughts and realize I haven't planned any farther, but Miss Lydia likely knew that about me by now. She didn't let it go so far as to let me start doubting myself. Or become afraid of what came next. She showed me kindness right up to her last breath.

It came a little less than two hours after I told her good night. She simply took a breath, and then she didn't. She stopped, that was all. With so little fanfare and with such peace you would wonder why all the fuss is made about it by the living.

I sat with her until I could bear to look away.

I've been up here in my pink bedroom all night memorizing the last five years. Writing it all down. Trying to digest every detail before something gets away and I lose any little bit of her. What I have now will need to last me from now on.

I thought she should have one last night at home. She deserves that. Come morning, soon now, I'll call Harlan to come say good-bye to her. He will appreciate that.

We'll tell them he woke me by knocking and that's when I found her.

And then it will all begin.

Life as I will come to know it.

An adventure I would not have been able to imagine five years ago, no doubt.

I'm nervous, but I'm not afraid. I know I will miss her with every fragment of my soul as long as I live. But I also know this: she left me with everything I need to live without her.

She left me knowing who I am without looking into anybody's mirror. She left me believing I deserve to be loved. She left me the ability to trust.

And that is worth more than anything in her will, more than all the money in the world can buy. That is her true legacy to me.

Sure as rain.

Acknowledgments

Thank you to the fine writers who read early drafts—Dan Roettger, Terrance Griep, and Mary Logue. Jennifer Flannery, thanks for being so good in every sense of the word. Eternal gratitude goes to Emily Meehan for breathing life into this book.

I recognize the good fortune that makes Dave Lybarger my friend as well as my favorite brother, and am grateful to our parents, Charlie and Anna Jean Lybarger, who never let me believe there was anything I couldn't achieve.

Barbara Felt and Pete Barber, your endless offerings of support speak of the pompitous of love. Thank you.

Charlie, my son, you make me want to be the best I can be, every day of my life. I'm so glad you picked me.

❧ ❧ ❧